THE LEGEND OF THE BLOODSTONE

BOOK ONE

THE EYE OF DISPARAGER

BRETT STUART SMITH

ISBN:	Hardcover	978-1-4828-9411-0
	Softcover	978-1-4828-9410-3
	Ebook	978-1-4828-9412-7

To order additional copies of this book, contact
Toll Free 800 101 2657 (Singapore)
Toll Free 1 800 81 7340 (Malaysia)
orders.singapore@partridgepublishing.com

www.partridgepublishing.com/singapore

For my Mother who would have loved to read the final story
and my aunty Daphne for all the years of inspiration.

Thank you to Theo for the unfaltering support,
Lesli for the initial faith in the process
and Errol for invaluable help with the editing.

Artwork—Diogo Lando

ABOUT THE BOOK

The three kingdoms of Alton Savia have lived in peace for generations; but now a dark force gathers in the North and threatens the Southern Alliance as rumours spread of the resurgence of the Order of the Obsidian Mask. Dorian longs to escape from the remote village he has known all his life and now a sudden turn of events catapults him into a strange and dangerous new world, a world of intrigue, magic and the unfaltering march of ten thousand men into battle. Who can turn the tide of war or is all hope lost in the face of unmitigated evil?

FOREWORD

I grew up in a world of turmoil and flux, finding an escape between the pages of a myriad Science Fiction and Fantasy novels. I lived on a diet of magic and wonder conjured up by Lewis and Tolkien before I was twelve and had devoured hardcore tech dispensed by Asimov, Aldiss, Heinlein and Herbert by the time I was fifteen. Thanks to my father's fascination with the genre and my great aunt's extensive collection, I have lived many lives and been transported to many weird and wonderful universes. My mind's eye had discovered a fertile incubator and before long, I was creating my own storylines and heroes. A disastrous turn of events in my life left me in a dark and lonely place and this unlikely crucible gave rise to The Legends of the Bloodstone. This is where one journey ends and another begins. The page is a canvas brushed with words and your imagination the palette.

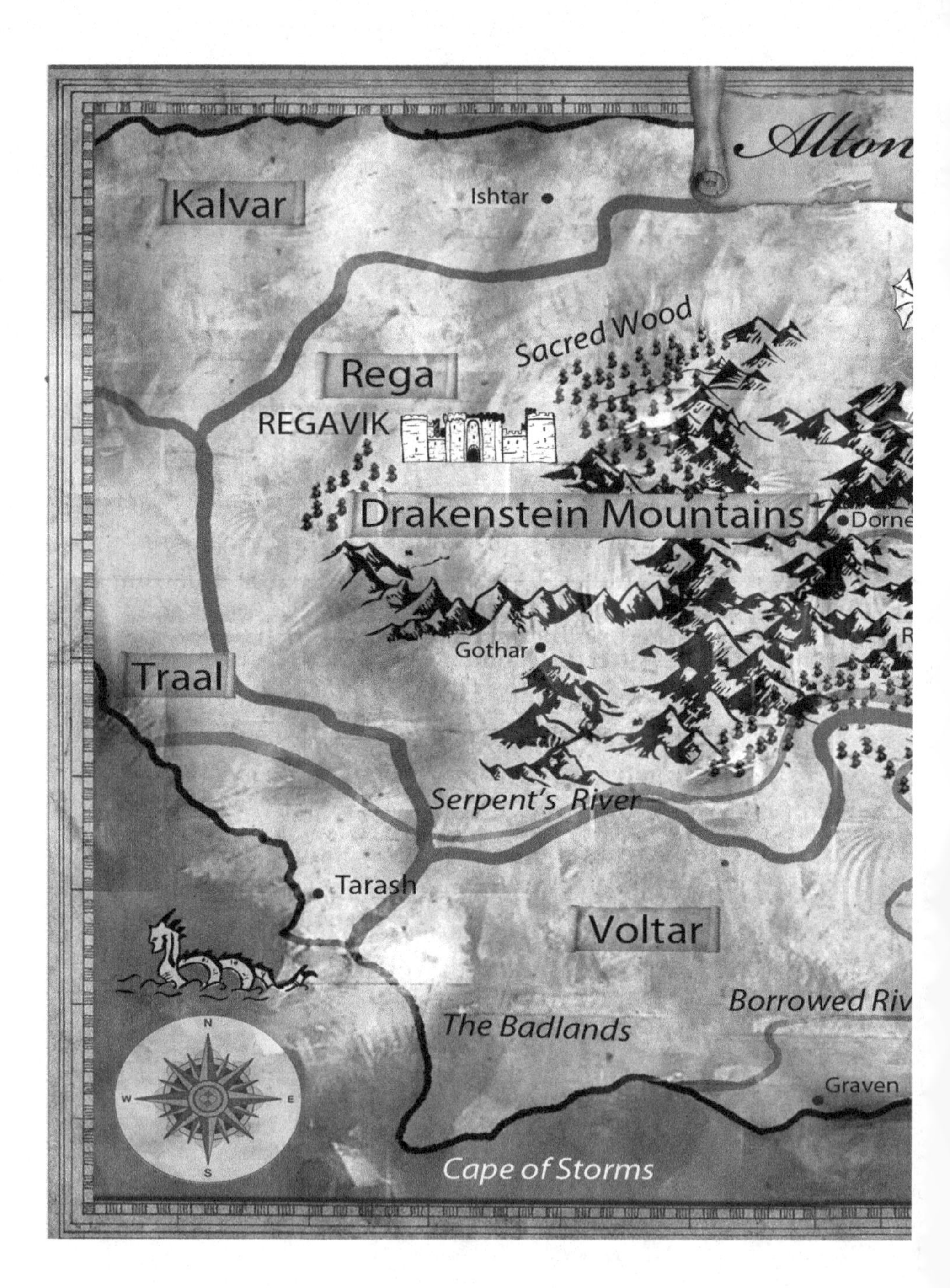

Alton
Kalvar
Ishtar
Sacred Wood
Rega
REGAVIK
Drakenstein Mountains
Dorne
Gothar
Traal
Serpent's River
Tarash
Voltar
Borrowed Riv
The Badlands
Graven
N
W
E
S
Cape of Storms

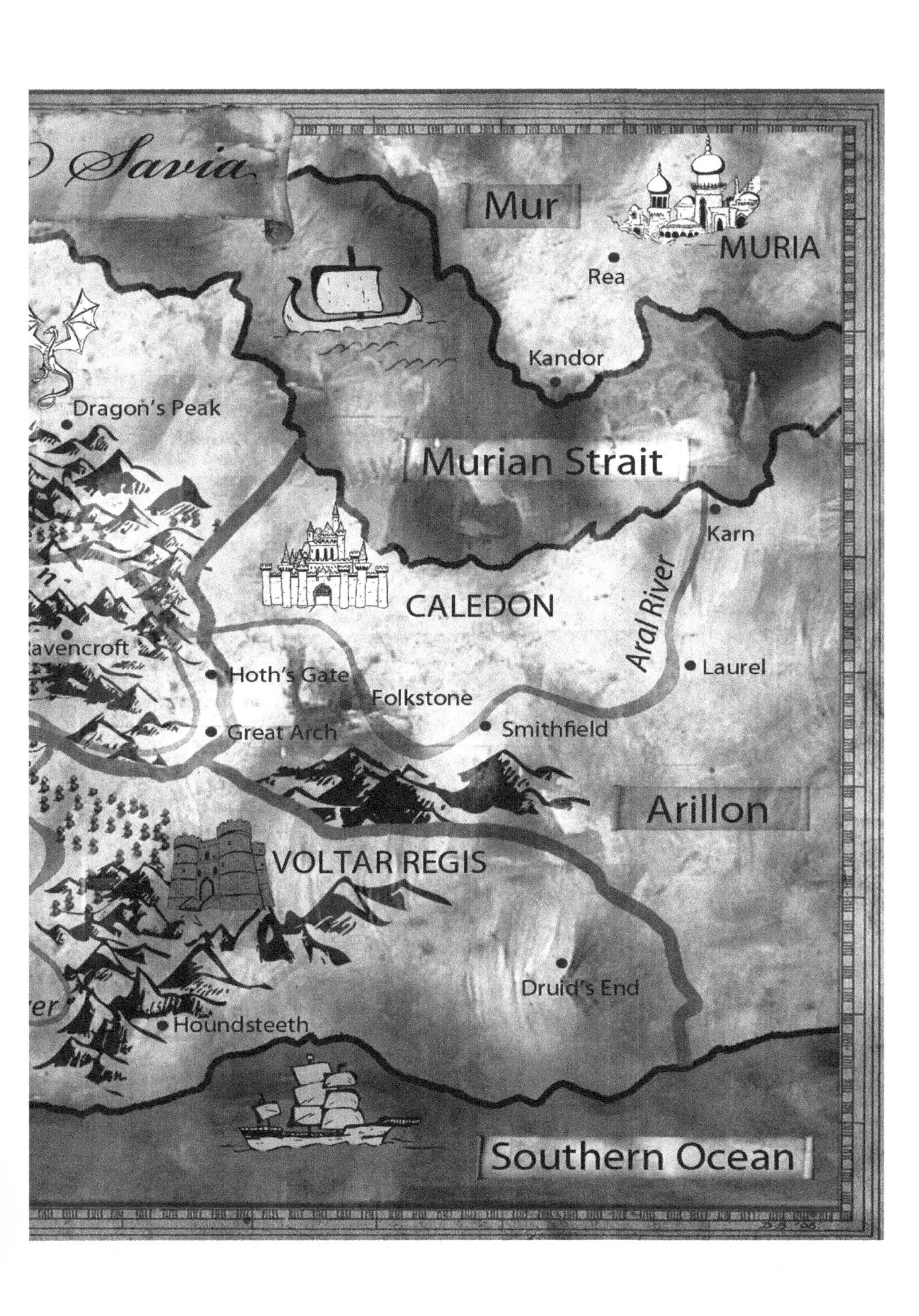

Savia
Mur
MURIA
Rea
Kandor
Dragon's Peak
Murian Strait
Karn
CALEDON
Aral River
Laurel
Hoth's Gate
Folkstone
Great Arch
Smithfield
Arillon
VOLTAR REGIS
Druid's End
Houndsteeth
Southern Ocean

CONTENTS

ONE

STRANGE TIDINGS

Dorian sat beneath the ancient leaning redwood surveying the distant horizon. The tree shied away from the ocean's constant onslaught. He tried to get comfortable; shifting about pressing his back into the perfectly moulded hollow, he had discovered when he was a very small boy. The sky pressed down, dark sacks heavy with imminent rain. Salt-laden wind lashed up the cliff face and tugged at Dorian's unkempt, blonde hair, whipping it about and catching him in his eyes, making them smart. He pulled his threadbare cloak more tightly about him and sniffed at the wind in exasperation, turning his attention to the waves that battered the rocks far below. Bad dreams had haunted him of late; glimpses of outlandish images surfacing in his mind, flickering towards the edges of his consciousness. He often came here to reflect upon them.

This was *his* private place. His escape from the mundane and adventure-less life, he had come to know and detest in the village. It was a quiet vantage point where he could survey his world and possibly catch a glimpse of a passing Voltarian galleon or, if he was lucky, a Kalvari carrack. Today there were no ships in sight and he was left to dwell upon his lot in life. His cousin had been irritating him again and he had had to get away for a desperately needed respite. It had been a trying day with Toby doing his utmost to get under Dorian's skin. He cast his mind back to the incident earlier in the day when the little twerp had deliberately soiled the freshly scrubbed floors that Dorian had spent hours working on; purely out of spite. They had nearly come to blows and he had mustered all of his willpower to avoid a confrontation that would have inevitably featured blood and a broken nose for Toby. Dorian always pulled away before he lost his temper. Toby enjoyed getting him into trouble and seemed to relish the chastisement Dorian would endure at the hands of Toby's father. Uncle Owen was Dorian's inherited guardian and could be quite hard on him at times, always cracking the whip and working him to the bone.

To his right the sheer cliff face continued as far as the eye could see. Many fingers of rock stitched the land neatly to the ocean and ranged away into the mist, sentries marking the rise and fall of the ocean. A chasm a hundred leagues from Graven broke this march southwards, where the desolate land disgorged the *Borrowed River* into the ocean. The mountain folk gave the river this name because it looked so foreign in the barren southern landscape. He glanced down to where the village of Graven crouched in the shadow of the keep. The sight of the squat stone buildings huddled together under the watchful eye of Graven Keep high above brought back a familiar sense of hopelessness. He just wanted to get away; to venture north beyond the keep and inland to the great city of Voltar Regis.

He had heard many tales about the capital of Voltar from the traders who visited his uncle's inn. Maybe he could run away and join the army to become a great warrior in the fight against the North. Then he could also attend the Festival of Mia, the Earth-Goddess, in Arillon. He had learnt about the festival in the great books on Alton Savia's tradition and culture and always longed to attend.

He would glean information from trading adventurers, who were rare this far south, when they came in overland with their caravans of pack mules. The sea was far too rough and the coastline too rugged for the mooring of trading vessels and the small bay in Graven was no more than a reef-bound inlet. The ships always sailed past Graven at a safe distance and carried on around the Cape of Storms in the far south. Dorian often wondered where the ships were heading and would pore over the maps Miss Lambourne provided for his lessons; these were always the highlight of his day. The days in between lessons sucked the life out of him and he would end up asking his uncle numerous questions, usually answered with a sharp retort and accompanied by a deft clip around the ear. This tack proving fruitless, he took to assailing his uncle's customers at the inn. More often than not, they too would be loath to say much, and would instead order him to fetch more food or wine. He had become accustomed to their toothless, lined faces slurring demands. Sometimes they just turned away completely from his incessant badgering.

It had been two months since a visitor had stayed at the inn and his uncle was in one of his bad moods, which induced a frightful scowl. He was a living body wearing a Voltarian funeral mask of clay. The clay set ever firmer with each passing week. He resigned himself to the fact that he would probably have to endure his uncle's morbid demeanour until the onset of spring. The prospect made him feel even more desperate. The narrow northern pass through the mountains was in the firm grip of winter, making it almost impossible to negotiate. This meant they would not be receiving any guests for quite a while yet. Thick ice, snowdrifts, and rock-falls were but a few of the perils facing the visitor who might brave the Houndsteeth this time of year. During the summer months, any traveller's trek to the southlands would take them along the coastal track through the badlands and on to Traal.

He was shaken from his daydream when he noticed a flickering orange glow from the Black Tower, the tallest in the keep, and he jolted upright as he suddenly realised the time. The evening watch had lit the flame that would burn until sunrise, warning passing ships of their proximity to the dangerous reefs and rocks below. He felt his stomach tighten as he imagined his uncle's reaction to his tardiness. In a flash, he sprang to his feet and careened down the steep slope towards the village.

Angry with himself for losing track of the time, he ran, almost tripping twice over the loose gravel. He was on an errand to collect a haunch of wild boar from the butcher at the edge of the village. He knew that he could never account for the hour or so he had spent daydreaming up on the cliffs. His mind raced as he tried to think of an excuse. Bursting into the butcher's shop he spluttered breathlessly, 'sorry, where is it—I must hurry, they will be waiting to start the dinner.' His chest was heaving.

'You're an edjit,' the butcher said, as he handed him the wrapped haunch, shaking his head. Dorian grinned and snatched the parcel. Leaving the shop, he headed towards the inn at the other end of Graven's single road.

As he approached the entrance to the two-storey building, he had a feeling that something was not right. He could not put his finger on it. He heard the creaking sign jostle on its chains above him, and looked up to see the eyes of *The Weary*

Traveller staring down at him disapprovingly. It was then that he noticed a light through an upstairs window. This was odd at this time of night as everyone would usually be downstairs and his uncle was adamant about not wasting oil. Dorian had half expected his uncle to be waiting on the threshold with a bullwhip in hand.

He entered the main hall and noticed his cousin Toby behind the gleaming oak counter Dorian had spent an hour waxing earlier in the day. His cousin's grubby fingers were drumming his irritation and Dorian eyed them, feeling a rush of annoyance. He contained himself and threw the wrapped meat on the counter. He walked over to the hearth and stretched his hands out welcoming the thaw. His whole body was frozen and he was glad to have his back to Toby, hoping he would disappear.

'Where the hell have you been gobshite?' barked his cousin. 'You've been gone over an hour. You're in big trouble an' you're definitely going to get it this time. We've been waiting to start the roasting an' we've got a visitor.'

'Who is it?' asked Dorian calmly.

'It's a messenger from the Baron an' he's here to see my father,' said Toby, snotty and aloof.

'Really, well who else would he be here to see . . . you?'

Toby grabbed the package, stuck his nose in the air, and turned on his heel, striding into the kitchen to prepare the meat for the griddle. He was a few months younger than Dorian and completely different in every way. Where Dorian was tall and robust, Toby was short and dumpy, much like his father Owen. Dorian was fair of complexion with shoulder-length, blonde hair, and hazel eyes. Toby on the other hand was sallow with dark, curly, short hair and dark eyes, one of them a lazy wanderer in his pudgy face. In fact, most people in the village and the keep, for that matter, resembled Toby. There was nobody else with Toby's one unique feature though and Dorian found his squinting eye quite disconcerting.

Dorian had always felt that he stood apart from the village folk of Graven and he was usually treated differently too. The villagers always gave him a wide berth and he was glad of it. Only the Baron had ever had a kind word for him. Baron Woodruff would descend upon Graven and invite Dorian to accompany his party on a hunt. This usually happened during the short summer months when the Baron would take his bloodhounds out on the chase through the woods in search of wild boar or deer. Toby abhorred these occasions and would always find a way to make Dorian regret them. The Baron taught Dorian how to ride and always allowed him to ride one of the smaller mares. Dorian knew his way around the woods and was quite a dab hand with a crossbow, proving him invaluable on their hunts.

Unusually the Baron had green eyes, and so he too was different, making him stand out much like Dorian. Dorian always thought the Baron understood what an outsider felt like, after all, he did have a title, and that certainly demanded special attention.

'So, 'ave you been up the mountain again laddie?'

Dorian had not noticed the blacksmith sitting at a table near the window. 'Well it's not really a mountain; it's a cliff, a mountain's much higher and . . .'

'What do you go up there for laddie?' asked the blacksmith with a mocking twinkle in his eye before Dorian could finish his sentence.

'My *name* is Dorian, and I go up there because I'm not afraid to,' he replied flatly.

There was a brief moment of tension and it looked to Dorian as if the old codger's bulging eyes were about to burst right out of his bald head. Footsteps on the timber staircase interrupted their bristly exchange and they both looked around to see who it was. Uncle Owen and a man Dorian had never seen before descended into the room. The stranger wore a blue tunic with an emblem of a white stag on his breast. It was the mark of a Voltarian soldier much like those seen on the breastplates of the men up at Graven Keep, but who was this person? Dorian knew every one of the Baron's staff, by face if not by name. The two men exchanged a few short words in deliberate, hushed undertones before the newcomer glanced fleetingly at Dorian and then bade farewell to the innkeeper. His black leather cape billowed behind him as he left the building.

'I thought he was staying for dinner?' Toby whined as he entered the room with the spiced boar carved up on a platter.

'Well he isn't. Now get that meat on the fire before we all starve to death,' snapped his father.

'But Dorian was late again, aren't you going to yell at him . . . it's *his* fault.'

'JUST DO AS I SAY BOY!' roared his father and then, to Dorian, in a more dulcet tone, 'go and fetch the wine and the bread lad.' Uncle Owen sat down at his usual table near the back of the room where it was warmest. His face was a picture of anguish.

Dorian walked behind the bar to the large vat and decanted the wine in amazement. He thought he dared not say a word lest the tide turn against him. A few more villagers entered the inn and sat themselves down in their usual places. Dorian carried the pitchers of wine over to the tables and began pouring the burgundy liquor out into the pre-set goblets. His uncle taught him this way. The heady bouquet of the wine made him feel ill; he could never understand why the customers loved it so much.

His uncle said nothing as he stared into the crackling blaze that licked the stonework in the fireplace. Something was wrong. What information had brought about this silence? What exactly had the stranger said? Uncle Owen was usually involved in an animated conversation with one or all of his customers by this time.

Dorian went to the kitchen to collect the bread. He then distributed it religiously before finally sitting down at his uncle's table. Dorian ate his bread quietly and watched as Toby came over to sit down opposite him with a look of sheer disdain on his face. The conversation at the other tables was low and everyone kept glancing over at Owen, expectantly.

Finally Marion, the butcher's wife and one of the few women in the village, bustled up to their table and said, 'I believe there's strangers come to the keep. I wonder what's going on up there. It's very odd having visitors this time of year . . . and who was the new messenger who came in here?'

'He accompanies a very important guest of the Baron,' said Owen carefully, 'he is a journeyman in the Baron's service.'

'Oh. Maybe it's to do with the strange rumours of evil folk come to the mountains,' she ventured. 'Or does he need *your* services then? Why, he didn't even stop to eat.'

There had been a lot of talk lately of the rise of an evil religion from the North, with the discovery of strange blood sacrifices in the woods. Hunters found mutilated rabbits with their blood dabbed in outlandish markings on the trees and stones in the vicinity. This was strange indeed, as food was hard to find in the dead of winter and even the hungry, wily mountain wolves had not touched the meat.

'Yes, in fact I have been commanded to take a barrel of my vintage Voltarian wine up to the keep on the morrow,' Owen said and left it at that. He did not want to elaborate and looked down at the table dismissively. Marion stomped off and immediately began relating her findings to the other villagers. Graven was quite isolated this time of year and visitors were something to talk about. Owen could hear Marion accentuating the "important guest" part of the tale and he thought that perhaps he had said too much. He would normally be as involved in the gossip as the next person would, but tonight his thoughts were elsewhere. Dorian and his cousin sat in silence until eventually Uncle Owen looked up and asked Dorian to begin serving the meat.

Dorian served the roast boar. The aroma now permeated the entire room and made his stomach churn in anticipation. He sat down and they all ate in silence, Toby still glaring at him with loathing. Finally, Uncle Owen started talking about the day's chores, reporting on how well the boys had fared with them. He reviewed their work at the end of each day. Today his uncle said nothing about Dorian being late again and so Dorian sat and listened quietly as his uncle rambled on. The cousins took turns in cleaning up after dinner and would usually go straight to bed afterwards. Tonight it was Toby's turn to wash up and so Dorian retired to his small room above the kitchen, at the back of the inn. He had shared a bigger room with his cousin when they were younger but as they grew older, it became increasingly evident that there was no love lost between the two boys.

Dorian had been in the care of his uncle and aunt practically since birth. They were his only living relatives. A mountain bear had killed his own mother and father in the woods one tragic summer. Dorian and his parents had been on their way to visit Uncle Owen and his wife Ruth. Dorian's father was Owen's brother and had been a hunter up on the mountain. His mother had been a foreigner and was fair of face, one of the main contributing factors to the rivalry between himself and Toby. People often mentioned how Dorian was blessed with his mother's good looks.

The story went that Owen became concerned when his family had not arrived at the expected time and went looking for them. He found Dorian crying in the woods near the lifeless, broken, and lacerated bodies of his parents. Owen was grief stricken and he took Dorian home for his wife Ruth to care for. Ruth was with child at the time and was able to nurse Dorian before she gave birth to Toby two months later. The gentle Ruth doted on the two boys and they vied for her attentions until sadly, she succumbed to an outbreak of the plague when they were only five years old. Owen was inconsolable and life had been extremely hard trying to bring up the two lads on his own. He did his best to look after them and had them schooled by a tutor who would come down from the keep once a fortnight laden with books. Dorian enjoyed the few hours he and his cousin spent with Miss Lambourne. To the boys she seemed old, but she was wise and very interesting to listen to. She would tell stories of faraway lands and the history of the three kingdoms. He most loved listening to her tales of her own adventures in Arillon and Rega. Dorian lamented the fact that he had to share Miss Lambourne's lessons with his cousin Toby who constantly wasted their time together with his dull interruptions.

Once they had reached puberty, Dorian had asked if he could move into the tiny storeroom above the kitchen on the pretext that Toby kept him awake all night with his snoring. His uncle agreed, much to Toby's chagrin, as Toby enjoyed tormenting his brooding cousin in any way possible and now felt deprived of his favourite pastime. Dorian was glad to have the little creep out of his sight. He was tired of the relentless badgering and bickering as it threatened to erode his sanity. Dorian was physically stronger than his plump, squinting cousin was and yet somehow felt he could not exert too much violence upon him. He had been close to breaking point on numerous occasions. Toby knew that Dorian would not hurt him but he also knew exactly how to pull all the right strings.

Dorian's temper was frayed and he felt that his leniency would soon yield to an uncontrolled outburst.

The cramped quarters and the stale, sweet smell were a small price to pay for the solitude and, in any event, it was much warmer here than the larger rooms despite the lack of a hearth or stove. He was drifting off to sleep while reflecting on the day's events, when he heard a sound at the door. Uncle Owen knocked and came in while Dorian sat up, alarmed at this unexpected intrusion.

'I need you to come with me at first light lad. We have been summoned by the Baron.' A shroud of concern hung over him.

'Up to the keep?' Dorian asked eagerly.

'Yes, up to the keep, that's what I said lad.'

'Do we have leave to *enter* the keep?'

'Yes, this time we do.'

'Why?' he ventured.

'Don't ask questions lad, you'll find out soon enough.' Uncle Owen left the room, ducking his head as he stepped through the low doorway.

Dorian sat and stared in disbelief. Why should he have to go *inside* Graven Keep? The guard always denied him permission to enter the keep in the past, despite him having asked on occasion. He had only ever been as far as the main gate. Dorian felt troubled as his imagination walked him through the great, much vaunted halls of the fortress. He had always wondered what secrets lay within the keep's walls and now that the opportunity presented itself, he felt apprehension. What was going on? This was strange indeed. He reflected on the evening's events. There had been the messenger, but he was a soldier or journeyman and he would surely not come from the keep just to order wine for a guest. No, there was something else afoot. What could it be? The request for wine was a ruse. Something important was about to happen and it had to involve *him* somehow. After all, Toby would usually be the one to accompany his father on this type of errand. Dorian could hardly contain himself and lay awake for an hour before he finally drifted off. He dreamt of rabbits and high walls but the overriding theme was a persistent feeling of restlessness. Was someone or something chasing him, or was he the pursuer? He could not tell, but a sense of urgency prevailed throughout. As the pale, cold light of dawn crept into his small room and the sound of distant seagulls whirling overhead infiltrated the gloom, he awoke in a sweat.

TWO

A PARTING OF WAYS

The morning arrived blustering and cold with an easterly wind howling in off the sea, tormenting the trees around Graven. They flailed in leafless protest like complaining women with nobody to take heed. Dorian scampered downstairs to wash himself, his bare feet blue with the cold. In the kitchen, he collected a kettle of boiling water from the fireplace and poured it into the stone basin containing freezing washing water from the day before. As he splashed his face with the warm water, he breathed in the steam that rose up to meet him, the smell of the oily soap all too familiar. He looked up when he noticed movement through the crude glass of the kitchen window. He went over to the back door and opened the top latch to lean out. He was surprised to see that his uncle had already hitched the donkey up to the cart and was busy rolling a barrel of wine out of the cellar. His uncle turned to him as he stood shivering in the morning air with his arms clasped tightly about his chest. 'Come on boy, we're going to be late. Get your cloak and boots on and make sure you bring a clean shirt.'

'I've only got one,' Dorian chortled raising his left eyebrow to frame a bemused expression.

'Well hurry up and don't give me lip boy,' said Owen as he rolled the barrel up onto the cart. The donkey shivered too and looked around at Dorian rather miserably. Dorian ran upstairs and threw on his shirt and pants. He collected his leather pouch and cloak that hung on the back of his bedroom door and on his way out he grabbed a potato from the larder; a gift for the forlorn looking ass.

'Here you go Rudder,' he said as he patted the animal's neck. Owen looked on blankly. Toby had appeared in the doorway to bid his father farewell. He completely ignored Dorian.

'Good-bye dear cousin,' Dorian said sarcastically as they made their way towards the steep road leading up to the keep. He looked back to see Toby stomp back into the inn with his nose pointed skywards in the usual manner. "What a haughty little runt," he thought.

'Come on then,' his uncle called. Dorian jumped up beside Owen and grabbed the reins giving them a flick to get Rudder started on their way up the hill.

They rattled out of the village and began making their way up the winding road that was very slippery this time of year. Rudder battled to find his footing as loose bits of shale scattered beneath his hooves.

Dorian jumped down, giving the reins to Owen, and helped the cart along as a gulley caught the wheel. At one point Rudder lost his footing altogether and they both had to alight for fear of losing control of the cart. His uncle could do little to help as Dorian wrestled with the laden cart for what felt like an eternity. He could feel the muscles in his shoulders bunching as he put his head down and heaved the cart over the rough patch of road. He was a strong young man; hours of physical labour and many years of climbing the cliffs had moulded his body into a well-honed stack of muscle.

It took them the best part of an hour to reach the keep's massive iron portcullis. They waited on the small bridge that spanned a deep crevasse below them. Dorian caught snatches of the sea's assault on the rocks far below, carried up to his ears by the relentless wind. He knew that this was a formidable fortress, which had guarded this part of the kingdom for centuries. It was only now that he realised just how effective the fortress must have been during the Onslaught of Traal two centuries before. The legends foretold that a last minute alliance between the reclusive mountain men of Rega and the armies of Voltar, under the then Baron of Graven, had held the northern pass and saved the Kingdom of Voltar from the marauding hordes of Traal.

'Who goes there?' a voice from above called out.

'It is I, Owen Barclay of Graven come in answer to the Baron's call,' was his faltering reply.

'Wait,' shouted the man as the unlikely pair looked at each other. His uncle's eyes were wide with an emotion Dorian had never seen before.

There was a raucous noise as they heard mighty chains rattle and scrape. The huge portcullis began to lift off the ground inch-by-inch finally exposing a long passage leading to heavy, hardwood gates strapped by steel girders at the other end.

'Proceed,' echoed the voice.

They passed through the gate and Dorian looked up to see the black, stone walls rise on either side to reveal a narrow strip of grey sky far above. All at once, he felt nauseated and reeled on his feet steadying himself against the wall. As his fingers touched the stone, he felt a tingling sensation through his fingertips and quickly recoiled in dismay. It was as if some bizarre force had emanated from the building itself and entered his hands like a frozen spider's web creeping up his forearms.

'Dorian, are you feeling alright?' his uncle asked turning to look at him.

'I'm fine. I just suddenly felt a bit sick, that's all.' He folded his arms under his cloak, tucking his hands under his armpits. The strange sensation lingered in his fingertips.

They reached the gates at the other end to hear the portcullis close behind them. A window opened to reveal a shrivelled up old face quizzically peering at them through the grille. The face disappeared and the opening was snapped shut. A moment later, the gates began to creak as they opened on their great hinges.

The old attendant who met them was familiar to the two newcomers. On occasion, his bony frame toiled through the village on some errand or other. He wore a full-length smock of black lamb's wool and looked up at them with bright, small eyes, which belied his age.

'Follow me,' he said leading them into a large courtyard.

A stable hand appeared and took Rudder by the reins, as another servant came to offload the barrel of wine. Dorian and his uncle stood and waited, not quite sure of what they were expected to do.

'Follow me,' the old man said again, 'your beast will be taken care of.' They followed the stooping figure as he shuffled across the courtyard with a bunch of silver keys jangling in his left hand. He stopped at a doorway on the other side of the courtyard and unlocked it with one of the keys revealing a broad flight of stone steps. 'Well up you go then,' he croaked.

Dorian wondered where they were going. This did not look like the way to the cellars. They should surely be heading down to the kitchens.

As they began the ascent, a gust of air from within warmed them. Dorian could smell the familiar scent of burning pine and it reminded him of the calluses on his hands. At the top of the stairs, they entered a cavernous hall lit by huge torches in iron sconces flanking the walls at regular intervals. It took a few minutes for their eyes to adjust to the interior light. It soon became apparent that elaborate dark tapestries hung between the circles of dancing light. These were expansive woven canvasses and, as the trio filed past, Dorian tried to fathom what it was they depicted. He looked up and noticed that the tapestries disappeared into a murky blackness far above.

"Dorian" a voice whispered eerily.

He looked about wildly. Again, that feeling of nausea took hold of his stomach, he felt dizzy, and it took all of his willpower to stay on his feet. His ears were ringing and again he heard his name.

"Dorian," it sang this time.

He kept walking and the feeling passed almost as quickly it had come over him. He had never felt anything like this before. It was peculiar, almost like a wave that washed over him, or through him. He tried to clear his head and thought he might be imagining both the feeling and the voice.

The pictures in the tapestries slowly became evident and he could see that a great battle was raging across the walls. They passed scores of hideously deformed faces, a myriad of bizarre weapons bristling amongst them. It was a vast army pushing ahead and as the trio reached another door at the other end of the hall, Dorian noticed a depiction of Graven Keep carved into its polished surface. The door opened silently to reveal a well-lit room with an enormous inglenook directly opposite them. A pile of logs crackled there and Dorian felt glad of the warmth. Above the mantelpiece hung an oil painting of a nobleman that bore a remarkable resemblance to the Baron. The noblemen stood victorious with a mighty sword held aloft and his right foot crushing the slain body of a hideous creature, half dragon, half serpent with bat-like wings broken and twisted. Sharp spines covered its head and it appeared to be in its death throes with a grimace of fangs reaching for its attacker.

The room was circular with four small doors arranged around the perimeter and a large round table at its centre. Three men sat at the far side; two of them rising to their feet as Dorian and his uncle entered.

Baron Barton Woodruff of Graven remained seated; the man to his left was a total stranger, while the soldier to his right was the messenger who had paid a visit to his uncle the previous evening. Both men wore the blue and white colours of Voltar.

'My lord, Owen and Dorian Barclay of Graven,' announced the old man who had escorted them, before he turned and trundled from the room. Dorian could not understand why they found themselves before the Baron and his strange new visitors. He began fidgeting with his shirtsleeves.

'Well met gentlemen,' said the Baron. 'Allow me to introduce Drake Arvin to my left and his brother Flynn to my right. They hale from Arillon.' They each bowed in turn. The newcomers were shocked as this was a sign of respect usually accorded people of high status only. They followed suit as would be expected in this customary form of salute. Dorian knew all about Arillon, the great kingdom that lay to the north of Voltar. He had met very few people from there and noticed that the two men were fair of complexion. Drake was tall and lean, with green eyes similar in colour to those of the Baron. He had a scar across his right eye, running the length of his cheek to his chin. His hair was short and blonde, interspersed with grey. Flynn was shorter than Drake with light brown hair and eyes that matched his hair colour. Both men wore broadswords and daggers at their sides. So, they were brothers. "There is a strange aura about these men," thought Dorian feeling uneasy.

The Baron stood up. 'I know this must seem strange to you, being summoned in this way, but . . .' he hesitated, 'there is a lot to be explained.' He looked at Owen now, 'suffice to say that you have served me well Owen Barclay and you will be rewarded handsomely for your endeavour. I must ask that you take leave of us now as your duty has been fulfilled.'

'Thank you m' lord,' said Owen as he bowed and turned to leave the room. He stopped and looked at Dorian. There were tears in his eyes and he walked up to Dorian and threw his arms around him. Dorian stood frozen and bewildered not knowing what was happening. His uncle had never expressed this kind of affection before. 'Good-bye my lad,' he said as he let go, his voice quivering. Dorian had never seen emotion like this in him before either and watched in shock as he walked away. Two attendants stood on either side of the doors and opened them for Owen as he left the room.

Dorian stood nervously before the three men, not quite sure of what to do. Why had the Baron sent his uncle away? This was extraordinary; suddenly, he felt very much alone.

'Please sit down,' said the Baron. The three men opposite him sat down together. Dorian slowly walked up to the table to sit on one of the leather chairs facing them. 'Well,' said the Baron, 'I don't know where to begin . . . there is so much to be said. Let me start by saying that much of what you know of your past, or more precisely your origin, is not as you have been led to believe.'

Dorian stared at him incredulously. 'What do you mean m' lord?' he mumbled.

'This will come as a shock to you, but the time has come for you to learn something of your true birthplace.'

'But I was born up on the mountain,' murmured Dorian, feeling like he had just been thrown down a well.

'Not exactly,' continued the Baron, 'you were born in Arillon and brought to Graven, here in Voltar, as a babe for safekeeping.'

'But my parents, they . . . safekeeping from what may I ask m' lord?'

'Ah. I know this is all a bit sudden, but all will be revealed to you in due course. It is important that you do not rush things Dorian. I have permission to impart only certain facts to you at this time. Much depends on you and your willingness to accept the truth.' He gazed at Dorian with an expectant look in his eyes.

Dorian was unsure of what to say and sat in silence looking from one man to another. 'Well what is the truth m' lord?' he asked, finally realising that they had been waiting on his response.

'It is important that I first explain the nature of the circumstances that have led to this point. There is much to tell and I am afraid I do not have sufficient time. Are you aware of the forces at work in this world?'

'I'm not quite sure what you mean m' lord,' said Dorian.

'The forces of good and evil?' asked the Baron carefully.

'Well yes, everybody knows that these forces are in existence m' lord,' answered Dorian tentatively.

'They exist on many levels Dorian. The average person has no inkling of these things. Our faith in the Earth-Goddess Mia teaches us of the great power of birth and creation, however, there are older Gods whose powers stem from the seeds of evil and destruction. These are both great forces which can be bent to the will of those with the ability to do so.'

'You mean magic m' lord,' said Dorian.

The three men at the other end of the table glanced at each other.

'Yes, well that is one way of putting it I suppose,' answered the Baron, 'although that is the name given to the use of this power by the common folk, Dorian. We up here prefer to call it *The Wielding*.'

'Wielding?' repeated Dorian, and as he did, a wave of nausea washed over him making his ears ring again. What was happening to him?

'You can feel it Dorian,' said the Baron. 'Some people are more susceptible to it than others. A lot has to do with your bloodline and the use of certain infused artefacts or objects.'

'What? I'm just feeling a little ill that's all, I didn't have any breakfast m' lord,' replied Dorian aggrieved. This was all becoming a little bit too much for him. He was not quite sure whether the Baron and the two brothers were making fun of him or just completely insane. He began to feel like a rabbit in a snare and started eyeing the perimeter of the room for a quick escape.

'Maybe we should have some breakfast, my lord,' said Drake in a jovial voice. He spoke for the first time amazing Dorian with his deep and resonant voice.

'Good idea, my man,' said the Baron as he got up and walked over to the mantelpiece where he pulled on a dark red chord. 'Let's have our breakfast; it is about that time now. Would you like to eat Dorian?'

Dorian always liked to eat and thought that despite the circumstances he could do with a hearty meal. It might make him feel better, more able to deal with the situation at hand. 'Yes please m' lord,' he said quietly.

Within minutes, the doors opened and three servants walked in bearing great silver trays laden with a selection of steaming dishes. They placed the trays on the table and went about setting plates and cutlery before the seated men. The Baron gave thanks to the Earth Mother, as was the custom. One of the servants then came and stood beside Dorian, looking straight ahead. After a second or two, she looked down at him as if he was supposed to say something.

'Um . . . that will be all thank you, we will serve ourselves,' said the Baron. The servants bowed formally and left the room. 'Help yourself Dorian.'

Dorian hesitated at first but then decided to tuck in and satisfy the ravenous hunger that nested in his stomach. There were all kinds of delicious things on offer, fried bacon and eggs, hot cinnamon buns with fresh butter, pastries with jam, dried fruit and a steaming pot of coffee to wash it all down. This was a veritable feast. The others waited, looking at him with interest for a few seconds but soon followed his example.

'I see you have a hearty appetite young man,' said the Baron. 'Good, you will need to build up your strength.'

'What do you mean m' lord?' asked Dorian with a mouth full of pastry.

'You are to leave at once for Ravencroft,' answered the Baron.

'Leave . . . what for? Where is Ravencroft?' asked Dorian swallowing hard.

'You must leave because it is not safe for you to remain here any longer. Ravencroft lies in the lower reaches of the Drakenstein at the junction between Voltar, Arillon, and Rega.'

'I am not safe, why . . . and what will happen to me at Ravencroft m' lord?' asked Dorian, starting to feel panic well up inside of him again.

'Don't be alarmed my boy, you will be accompanied by these two men here. They are good men in the service of a great friend and ally of mine,' assured the Baron.

'But I thought they were in your service. They are wearing the colours of Graven Keep,' said Dorian.

'They often wear the colours of various houses. The nature of their work requires that they do not draw undue attention to themselves. There are many eyes watching the movement of men throughout the Southern Alliance these days,' said the Baron, with concern.

'Who do these men serve?' asked Dorian.

'They are in the Service of Morgan the Free of Ravencroft. He has been instrumental in safeguarding the security of Alton Savia and maintaining the peace and stability of the Three Kingdoms. I suppose you could say that they serve all of us really. Our alliance is once more under threat, but this time it is a more insidious enemy that infiltrates the very fabric of our society. A complicated and convoluted story . . . um . . . let me explain a little of our history to you. You have no doubt heard of the Onslaught of Traal?'

'Yes my lord,' stated Dorian.

'The Ruler of Traal became a powerful Wielder of the forces I mentioned earlier. He had found the Helmet of Darkness, also known as the Obsidian Mask, an ancient and very powerful artefact that has been in existence since our first historical records began. People believed that it had been forever lost in the great Southern Ocean, but it called to the Traalian king, driving him to find it. He sent many men to a watery grave in his quest before finally discovering the mask. Unfortunately, he was not pure in heart and swayed to the side of the forces of darkness. He had a thirst for power and became inflamed with a passion to conquer the whole of Alton Savia, driving his armies to madness, in an attempt to do so. As you know, we held him back and crushed his armies before they could enter Voltar. The people of Traal were all but destroyed by famine and disease and now they live in small settlements scattered far to the south.'

'What has all of this got to do with me my lord?' asked Dorian.

'The helmet disappeared just after the battle, before it could be destroyed and its power has recently been felt in the far northern land of Mur. It is now in the hands of the Empress. We believe she is planning an invasion of Alton Savia, despite or perhaps because of, her alliance with King Dragar. We believe Dragar is secretly conspiring to form a military alliance with Mur and turn brother against brother. Things have been going from bad to worse in Arillon and we fear Dragar is fomenting a civil war as a precursor to his greater ambitions. There are still those in Arillon who owe their allegiance to the alliance of the three kingdoms of Alton Savia and have rebelled against Dragar's rule. The citizens of Arillon have stirred up old rumours that he gained the throne through murder and deception. Rega has joined our cause once more to keep the forces of evil at bay, possibly even destroy them once and for all.'

'There is a rotten heart on the throne in Arillon that threatens to tear the Three Kingdoms asunder,' said Drake sadly.

'You play a very important role in all of this in that your line of descent has empowered you with an ability which is now needed by the Southern Alliance,' said the Baron, looking at Dorian seriously.

'WHAT ARE YOU TALKING ABOUT?' Dorian cried, standing up and banging his fists on the table rattling the silverware.

'Calm down Dorian, sit down, please don't get upset. I know this must be very difficult for you, but it is important that you learn these things in good time.' The Baron spoke in a soft tone and walked over putting his hand on Dorian's shoulder. 'There is something your father wanted you to have . . .'

'But who *is* my father?' asked Dorian desperately.

'Maybe he is not ready yet, my lord,' said Flynn speaking for the first time.

The Baron turned to him and said, 'There is no time left to waste Flynn. We must present him with it now or all might be lost.'

Dorian tried to clear his thoughts and looked at the three of them trying to decide if what was happening was real or just a dream from which he could not awaken. He had come here to deliver a barrel of wine and now in an instant his life turned upside down. Even though he had foreseen some event on the horizon, he felt angry, as he had not expected anything as outrageous as this. Yet at the same time, he also felt excited at the prospect of leaving this godforsaken hole.

Finally he said, 'if I am to understand you correctly, I'm not who I think I am and you can't tell me who my real father is but you want me to have something of his?'

'There are good reasons for this Dorian and they will soon be explained to you in more detail.'

'When is soon?' he asked.

'When you get to Ravencroft,' answered the Baron.

'I see,' said Dorian, with a note of resignation, 'what is this thing my *father* wanted me to have then m' lord?'

The Baron breathed a sigh of relief and walked over to one of the small armoured doors immediately to his right. He unlocked it and disappeared into a darkened chamber beyond.

THE TAMULUS OF ARILLON

Dorian sat with Drake and Flynn silently watching him. He still could not believe what was happening to him. This was an intriguing turn of events. He had felt a sense of detachment from the world around him for much of his young life and knew deep down inside that, one day, he would escape the confines of the village to seek adventure beyond the mountains. It was all so unreal, like a story told by his tutor where he was the main character. He thought that he heard his name being called again and turned to look in the direction of the doorway, expecting to see the Baron there, but he was nowhere in sight.

'What is wrong?' asked Drake.

'I thought I heard my name being called,' said Dorian, confused looking about as if to identify the originator. Just then, the Baron appeared carrying a small delicately crafted case in his hands. Again, Dorian heard his name and realised he *felt* his name called rather than hearing a voice actually call out to him. It was like a lingering whisper. 'There it is again, I've heard it before,' he said.

'What have you heard Dorian?' asked the Baron placing the small veneered box on the table.

'I think it's calling him, my lord,' said Drake.

'I thought it might,' said the Baron. He took a small silver key out of his pocket, unlocked the case, and opened the lid.

Dorian felt another wave of nausea wash over him. It was much stronger than before and he clutched at his stomach thinking he might spew. The Baron lifted a glittering chain out of the container. He held it up to the light. A small round amulet of gold hung before them with strange ornate designs engraved on its shining surface. In the centre lay a golden scorpion surrounding a ruby with a hue of deep red blood. It glowed with an inner light. Its presence filled the entire room and everyone looked at it in awe.

'Behold the Tamulus of Arillon,' said the Baron reverently.

Dorian could certainly feel its presence. It emitted a tangible strength that drew him towards it. He tried to pit his will against the instinct to draw closer to it, but the more he tried to resist, the stronger the force became and he found himself walking over to where the Baron stood.

'It is yours Dorian of Arillon,' said Baron Woodruff as he placed the amulet around Dorian's neck. Dorian felt burdened with a great weight. His whole body tingled and his mind became unfocused. It was that same sensation he had felt earlier in his fingertips and hands, but it was greatly amplified now and it rushed through him like wildfire making him feel both hot and cold at the same time. He felt himself slowly sinking into an abyss of darkness and silence. The world around him closed in, he felt a great peace descending upon him like a warm dream in the arms of the Goddess Mia, and then in an instant he felt a cold sharp probing. An evil force was seeking him out. It shrieked and howled around him and he turned from it in fear. He tried to will himself as far away from it as possible and as quickly as it had arrived, it was gone. It was as if he had shut some unseen door and become invisible to its cold tendrils. He heard the Baron's voice but it sounded like he was far away, ' . . . don't wrestle with it Dorian.'

His mind began to clear and he came to his senses only to find himself lying on the cool slate of the floor.

'Are you alright my boy?' asked the Baron standing over him, the faces of Drake and Flynn peering over his shoulder.

'I think so,' said Dorian. 'What happened, it felt like I was whisked away? I felt something terrible searching for me . . . or . . . reaching out for me. It was horrible.'

'It's the Empress. She must be wearing the helmet. It gives her the ability to see. She is trying to find him, there's no time left, we must leave at once, and make for Ravencroft,' said Drake. He turned to the Baron, 'We must get him to Morgan as soon as possible so that he can instruct him in the ways of the Wielding. He must learn to protect himself. It won't be long before she finds him.'

'The Tamulus should shield him from her prying eyes,' said the Baron, 'but for how long I cannot tell, she gains in strength with each passing day. You are right; it is not wise to dally any longer. I will instruct my staff to pack for you and prepare the horses at once.'

'I'm not sure I'm ready for the *Wielding*,' Dorian said, and then, 'who exactly is this Morgan?' Drake helped him up and onto a chair.

'Morgan the Free is an advisor to and friend of the Southern Alliance. He is very powerful in the ways of the Wielding and has instructed many champions and even Kings in its arts,' said Drake.

The Baron hastily walked over to the servant's chord and summoned the old man who entered the room shortly afterwards. He gave the old man instructions to prepare the journeymen's horses as well as his own steed Fire, which Dorian would ride. Dorian knew the Baron was very fond of his trusted mount, as Dorian had witnessed them together many times. Fire was a huge thoroughbred with a shining black coat and a mind of his own. He bit the occasional stableman and they gave him a wide berth.

'You are going to need a better pair of boots and warmer clothes young man,' said the Baron, 'come with me and we will find some for you.'

He followed the Baron, leaving the other two men behind in the circular room.

As they walked through a maze of dark passages lit by sputtering torches, Dorian became aware of the sheer size of the fortress. He tried to fathom when the keep had been built and by whom. It was obviously centuries old and yet it was still intact, as if it had just been finished. In an instant a picture of hundreds of short sturdy men, wearing apparel he did not recognise and chiselling rock out of the mountain, popped into his head. He stopped in disbelief, totally surprised by this random thought.

'What is it?' asked the Baron.

'I don't know, I just had the strangest vision of dwarves cutting rock from a mountain,' said Dorian.

'What were you thinking of at the time?' asked the Baron.

'I was wondering when the keep was built and by whom.'

'Well there you are, it's the Tamulus,' said the Baron. 'It will give you certain gifts Dorian, which you must use wisely. The affect is different for each person who wears the Tamulus. It is never certain how exactly it will work, as its power is dependent on the wearer and the nature of his or her character.'

'Can anyone wear it?' asked Dorian.

'Certainly not; many people have perished just by attempting to wear it! The forces of nature infuse this charm and can be very destructive if not meant for the person. The Tamulus and its bearer are destined for each other by lineage. Nobody knows how this was decided; it just unfolds as it was meant to be.'

'How did you know it was meant for me?' asked Dorian.

'It is written,' said the Baron turning from Dorian and continuing down the dimly lit passage.

Dorian once again fell in step behind the Baron. His mind was swimming with questions. 'Written where?' he asked.

'There is a lot you must still learn Dorian. Morgan the Free will answer all your questions when you arrive at Ravencroft. There is not much more I can tell you right now, I'm afraid.'

Dorian remained silent as they turned a corner and began climbing a winding staircase. He could not understand why the Tamulus had shown him the dwarves and yet kept silent about so many other questions that raced through his mind. He looked down at it and its beauty again struck him. He took it in his hand and noticed how the torchlight reflected in the stone. The depth and colour took his breath away as he had never held anything as precious as this in his life before. He stared into the crimson depths and felt a new longing and loneliness he did not quite understand. He began to feel a strong bond with this jewel, it was *his* now and he felt a strong urge to protect it.

Dorian and the Baron reached a small door and entered a bedchamber with a large bed to one side. The bed, constructed of a dark wood, had a post at each corner. Above the bed hung a tapestry depicting a hunting party making its way through the woods. Dorian noticed that one of the riders in the picture was Baron Woodruff astride his mighty steed, Fire. On another wall hung three portraits, but one in particular caught his eye. A picture of a beautiful young maiden, with a shock of hair the colour of burnt amber and beguiling deep blue eyes, stared out at him. 'Who is she?' he asked.

'Who?' asked the Baron as he opened a large wardrobe opposite the bed and started rummaging through some clothes.

'The girl in the portrait,' answered Dorian.

'Oh . . . that is a relative of mine. Gwyneth of Voltar, princess and heir to the throne . . . beautiful isn't she?'

'Yes m' lord, she is,' said Dorian mesmerised.

'And a handful too . . . she is always causing trouble for her father King William who constantly wants to pull his hair out because of her. A feisty young thing is our Gwyneth,' he said with a smile. 'Now where are those boots?' He continued to delve among the pile of garments in the wardrobe.

Dorian pulled himself away from the gazing eyes and walked over to a small shuttered window to look out at Graven. They were high up in the keep, overlooking the village and its small fishing bay. Beyond it, he could see the crested waves crashing over the reef. The morning sun lay behind a blanket of thick cloud. He gazed down at the village where smoke rose from the chimneys and realised that things would never be the same again. He could also see the inn from here and imagined his cousin going about his daily chores. He felt a pang of emotion but it passed in the blink of an eye.

'Here we go,' said the Baron, 'these should fit you.'

Dorian snapped out of his reverie and turned to the Baron who stood before him with a pair of leather boots in one hand and a cloak and a shirt in the other. He took them gratefully from the Baron and sat on the bed to change his boots.

'Thank you m' lord,' he said, rather sheepishly. The new boots were of soft leather and very comfortable with strong thick soles. He marvelled at their quality and felt somewhat embarrassed about the state of his old boots, as they were soiled and full of holes. He stood up, changed his shirt and the Baron helped him with the cloak when he had finished. It was dark blue and surprisingly heavy even though it was finely woven, soft to the touch on the inside and more durable on the outside. The Baron fastened the metal clasp at his neck. He noticed the Tamulus hanging there.

'I think it would be wise of you to wear this under your shirt,' he pointed at the Tamulus, 'you don't want to draw undue attention to it at this stage.'

'Yes m' lord of course,' said Dorian, slipping the amulet underneath his new white shirt.

'Well, you do look fine,' said the Baron with a broad smile on his face. 'Oh, I nearly forgot something . . .' He walked over to a large chest and opened it to burrow for something within. 'You may need this,' he said, once he found what he was looking for, 'keep it out of sight too.' He handed Dorian a small leather pouch, which upon inspection proved to be full of silver coins.

'I don't know what to say,' said Dorian, his eyes wide. He had never seen so much money at one time.

'No need to say anything my boy. I really should stop calling you 'boy,' the pleasure is mine Dorian of Arillon.'

Dorian liked the sound of that. He much preferred it to the multitude of condescending names people called him in the past; even *boy* was not that bad.

'We must get back to the others now. I'm sure they are anxious to depart,' said the Baron as he led the way out of the room.

'Who exactly are Drake and Flynn?' asked Dorian as he followed him out and down the stairs.

'They have been in the service of the House of Arillon for most of their lives, under the guidance of Morgan. They work to secure the sovereignty of the Southern Kingdoms now,' said the Baron as he quickened his pace.

Dorian wanted to ask about the House of Arillon, but for some reason thought better of it and followed in silence.

Drake and Flynn were deep in conversation when they returned to the circular room. They stopped abruptly and stood up when Dorian and the Baron entered.

'I think we should leave as soon as possible, if we are to make it through the Houndsteeth before nightfall,' said Drake, 'from there it's at least another three days hard riding to Ravencroft.'

'I agree,' said the Baron, 'let's make our way down to the stables.'

At the stables, the old man with the keys and three servants who had prepared rations for their journey greeted them. The hands brought their horses and Dorian was a little nervous of Fire, who snorted and stamped his hooves restlessly.

'Now, now . . . behave Fire,' said Baron Woodruff, patting the big stallion's flank. He whispered something in the horse's ear and he immediately calmed down. 'Don't be afraid of him Dorian, he's a big show-off, but he'll be fine when he gets to know you better. Come here and give him one of these sugar lumps.' The Baron took a bag of them out of his pocket and handed them to Dorian.

Dorian placed one in his hand and held it up spreading his fingers. 'There you go,' he said as the horse nibbled at it, stamping his hind legs as he did so. He eyed the bag as Dorian placed it in his leather pouch. Dorian noticed a well-made Voltarian crossbow and a mercenary sword placed in his saddlebag.

Drake walked up to Dorian and handed him a small, sheathed dagger. 'Hopefully you may not have to use this,' he said, 'but I would prefer you carried it.'

'Thank you,' said Dorian, taking it from him and fastening it to his belt.

The Baron asked Drake and Flynn to follow him. They walked a few paces away from Dorian and stood talking for five minutes. Dorian could not make out what they were saying as their voices were low but Drake was nodding his head every now and then. Finally, they came back and the Baron walked up to Dorian while the other two went about tightening their saddle straps.

'You can trust these men Dorian, they have been sent to escort you safely to Ravencroft. Take care of yourself and stay close to them.' The Baron looked him straight in the eye and he could see his concern.

'I will,' said Dorian, 'and thank you once again for your generosity m' lord.'

'There is nothing more to be said. You are to leave through the north gate,' said the Baron, 'and Godspeed.'

They mounted their horses, Drake and Flynn hoisting themselves into the saddles with ease. Drake's horse was a well-muscled, tawny stallion and Flynn rode a grey mare. Dorian found it a little more difficult to get into his saddle and one of the servants had to help him. They said farewell and guided their mounts through the archway that led to the back of the keep where the great iron portcullis rolled open for them as they approached. Before Dorian knew it, they were breaking into a canter on the dirt track that wound up the side of the mountain, Drake in front and Flynn behind. Before them, the Mountains of Rega ranged in the distance, the snow-capped peaks a flash of orange and pink as the winter sun climbed further into the cerulean sky. Dorian looked back over his shoulder to see the Baron and his attendants waving their farewell as the towers of Graven Keep disappeared from view.

THE PRINCESS OF VOLTAR

Voltar Regis stood at the heart of the Kingdom of Voltar, east of the Borrowed River and south of the mountains of Rega. A large and formidable stronghold with gigantic stone buttresses stood stark against the sky. This was farming country and the citadel stood tall, overlooking the surrounding villages. This had been the seat of power in Voltar for many generations and King William Cairn was the thirteenth regent of his lineage to hold the throne. His people loved him dearly and there was a strong kindred spirit amongst them, which was borne of generations of loyalty to his family. This kingdom was the breadbasket of Alton Savia and exported wheat and barley to both Rega and Arillon. The populace prospered under the dispensation of this court and now their wellbeing was again under threat from afar.

Gwyneth peered out of her chamber window high up in the south tower of the great fortress. A cold wind blustered across the steely flagstones below and people leaned into the blast as they moved about. She recognised many of her servants as they forged their way across the courtyard. Up above her the blue and white colours of Voltar flapped noisily from the parapets as kites swooped and taunted in and out of them.

She was feeling grumpy today. She was not the type of person who took no for an answer and her father's chastisement and dismissal earlier in the day played on her nerves. She cast her mind back to the last heated conversation with King William. 'Why should I stay behind when all able-bodied souls get ready for the march?'

'Because I am King and you are my daughter, the princess of Voltar, and not a soldier. I told you to go with your Mother but you would not listen and now you will have to stay here where it is safer for you,' answered her father.

'But my aim is better than most of that *rabble*,' she blurted.

'Nobody is arguing the point and I would remind you that you are referring to my army!'

'An army that would be all the stronger with my aim,' she retorted, smiling hopefully to soften the king's resolve.

'My word on this is final. You shall remain behind under the watchful eye of Tarrant here.'

Gwyneth had noticed Tarrant skulking in the background and loathed the sight of him. In her opinion he was a dubious priest and advisor and far too big for his boots. She had no time for the balding, hook-nosed acolyte who hailed from the North. He was always bowing and scraping, the eternal sycophant.

'Oh that should be charming,' she let the words slither from her tongue, 'can't wait!' She turned with furrowed brow and ran from the room, barely catching some of her father's words to Tarrant about keeping an eye on her. He was to ensure a guard be assigned to watch her every move.

"We shall see about that," she thought to herself.

Gwyneth spent the day sulking in her chambers with a guard posted at the door by her newly appointed keeper.

There was some noisy activity in the courtyard below as the gates lifted to let a messenger through. This had been commonplace of late, with messengers regularly riding back and forth between Voltar and Rega. There had also been a lot of raven activity but using the birds for messages was not always the safest option these days. She tried to peer through the frosted panes of her lofty window but could not see much and set the shutters slightly ajar to get a better look at the commotion below. A grey rider had entered the courtyard. "There is something different about this one. Too graceful in the way he dismounts and a glint of something below the hood. Got to find out more about him," she thought, "as if they can keep me prisoner in my own castle. Pah!"

She walked over to the door and peered through the keyhole. The fat guard still sat there, stuffed into a chair, seemingly asleep. She walked over to the bow-fronted bureau and made a din by banging her water jug about before going back over to the keyhole to see if there was any response. The guard was sitting upright peering at the door.

'Ah,' she feigned a sigh, 'I think I shall take a nap for the chill outside seeps into my bones.' She made a big fuss of jumping onto the bed so that it creaked and scraped over the floor. Taking off her shoes, she tiptoed back to the keyhole, quiet as a mouse. The guard was back in his comfortable position, eyes closed. She tiptoed over to her wardrobe and took out a hooded cloak, flinging it over her head. She also donned a pair of soft boots and then climbed inside the wardrobe, gently closing the door behind her. The cloak was one she had stolen from a washing line months ago. It was an old grey and patched servant's cloak that proved to be a good disguise. Inside the dark cupboard, she felt about for the lever she knew so well and in one swift movement was through into the secret passage behind the wall.

Her hands slipped along the cold walls until she found the sconce and gently removed the torch. In the darkness, she fumbled for the flint hidden in her robes and took a few steps before the yellow flame sprang to life and cast long shadows around her. She lifted the torch high above her head so that she could see the steps as she glided down the curved stairwell. At a point up ahead the secret passage ended at a little door that gave out into the main tower passage. It lay behind a heavy draped curtain. She waited at the door, catching her breath, and listened intently with her ear against the old timber.

Nothing!

The coast was clear and after dousing the torch and surrendering it to the flagstones; she slipped through the door like a phantom, waiting a moment behind the dark purple velvet. It was time to cross the passage and without much effort, she darted to the other side and made her way to the main door.

She was out of the main passage in a flash and found her way into the servant's access at the side of the great hall where she knew her father would be meeting with his newly arrived guest. She passed a scurrying servant, keeping her head down making as if she too were on some important errand. The servant ignored her. Good! The whole fortress had been abuzz with activity lately. She made her way to the vestibule behind the throne room and became aware of footsteps behind her, out of sight but just within earshot. Was someone following her? Her blood went cold and she quickly nipped behind one of the arches. The footsteps came closer and then hesitated a moment just nearby, as if the person had stopped to listen for something.

There was a deep inhalation of a breath and off they went again in a hurry. For a moment, she thought she recognised the gait, a shuffle, and a limp. "Yes," she thought, "it was that bastard Tarrant." She shuddered at the thought that he may be aware of her movements. A few moments passed before she decided it was time to make her move.

Her father was in the antechamber assigned for private meetings and she could hear the muffled sound of a conversation beyond the door. There were guards posted on either side so she hung back in the shadows and decided instead to head for the hidden vantage point beyond the apse. This was a secret space known only to the royal family, normally where one of them would be hiding in order to keep an eye on the proceedings, without the guest being aware that anyone watched them. She remembered a time when her mother, resplendent in court attire, had brought her here when she was very young. Gwyneth found the latched door and tiptoed into the recess behind the panelled wall. She peered into the darkness and as her eyes adjusted, she could see the filtered lamplight through the trellised panel, spill into this secret enclosure. Up ahead she realised that the light caught something shiny. "What is that?" she thought. "By the stars, it is a nose."

The realisation hit her squarely in the stomach; it was Tarrant.

"That squealing pig," he was hiding here too and spying on his master. Her father had received journeymen in private of late and she wondered how he had come to know of this secret place. What a treacherous villain he was and how she would love to accost him right now. However, she heard the conversation in the adjoining room clearly, now commanding her attention. Tarrant had not seen her, so intent was he on the proceedings. She held her breath and listened.

' . . . and you are certain of this?' her father was asking.

'Yes my Liege. The signs are there and I have read it in the stars. He has been found and makes for Ravencroft.'

Gwyneth had heard that voice before, many years ago when she was but a young girl and it was so familiar, warm and deep.

'He wields the power?' her father asked.

'We are not certain yet, but I must make haste to meet them by nightfall two days hence. I will assess his abilities then and tell him of his birthright when the time is right.'

'How many have knowledge of this development?' asked the king.

'The Brotherhood alone and none other my lord,' was the answer. 'We endeavour to keep this a secret in these dark times.'

'Yes, the enemy must not come to hear that the prophecy which foretells its demise may yet be realised. What of the armies Morgan?' the king asked.

It was Morgan. Yes now it all made sense: Morgan the Free. He was an old friend of this court and had been instrumental in bringing many projects to fruition in the kingdom. He had last been here ten years before and she remembered playing with his long hair and marvelling at his twinkling beads.

'Word has been dispatched and we march for Caledon through Hoth's Gate in the Drakenstein, hopefully a few days after you my Liege. It may be sooner depending on how we fare with the mission at hand. I have just come from Regavik where I held council with the king of the Mountain Men. He too is mobilizing,' said Morgan, 'his army shall join your forces in the foothills beyond the gap as agreed.'

'I too shall set forth within days,' her father added. 'I shall hold council with my captains tonight and we shall set off by first light on the fourth day from now. My men are almost ready. This is an expensive undertaking. We have been preparing but there is still much to do.'

'Yes King Mogador of Rega too has lamented at the sacrifice his Kingdom is making to launch this war,' said Morgan.

'I pray that it is not in vain. We shall wait in the foothills at the edge of the Sacred Wood for his arrival and yours.'

'What of our Queen my Liege, I was hoping to enjoy the pleasure of her fair countenance on this visit?'

'I have despatched her to her sister at Druid's End in the east. She will be safer there.'

'What of the Princess Gwyneth Sire?' Morgan asked.

'She would not go and vexes me still,' answered the king.

'To be expected my Liege,' Morgan said sympathetically, 'I will meet you in the foothills before Caledon.'

She heard chairs moving. They were concluding the meeting and she quietly melted from the hideout and moved swiftly in the direction of her sleeping chamber. Tarrant had not been aware of her but she had certainly smelt him. She thought of him as a sewer rat with an odour to match. Her father had to know of this treachery. Why was he spying on his own lord? Perhaps her father had asked him to witness this meeting; however, she thought this idea rather foolish. Surely, her father did not trust him enough to make him privy to the secrets of the Brotherhood of Guardians. "This needs further investigation," she thought.

Back in her chamber, she set about packing a small bag with a few victuals she had been hoarding for days. She wrapped cheese, bread and some salted meat in cloth and retrieved some fruit and nuts from a drawer. As she was hiding her provisions under the bed, she heard a sound at the door. Jumping onto the bed, she pretended to be asleep.

It was Ruby, her maid-in-waiting come to attend to her for dinner. 'Is m' Lady ready to be dressed for the evenin' meal,' she asked as she came in and stood at the foot of the bed. Ruby was plump and cheerful with rosy cheeks in a full moon of a face. Gwyneth was quite fond of her.

'Oh yes, I am famished,' she smirked, 'what with practically being locked up in the tower like a criminal. They are watching my every move you know, as if I would do anything untoward.'

'Well m' Lady needs protectin' doesn't she, what with all the talk of war and men running hither and thither,' said Ruby, sporting her signature toothless smile, 'no place for a princess to be runnin' about alone.'

'Come now Ruby, you know full well that I am more than capable of looking after myself,' retorted Gwyneth as she let Ruby help her into her evening attire. Ruby could not help but notice the small dagger close to her mistress's bosom as she dressed.

'What need have you of that m' Lady?' she asked mildly.

'Ruby you should know me by now. I must have something close to my heart at all times,' she answered, with a mischievous glint in her eye.

'Most young ladies would be holdin' a token of their esteem for a handsome young man there, not a dangerous weapon m' Lady.'

'That I know, but alas I do not have such a promising young prince snapping at my heels as you well know.' Gwyneth winked.

'Ah, but you would if you behaved more like a princess and paid more attention to the suitors that come a callin,' said Ruby, trying to sound older than her years.

'Hah! What rot! There has never been one to take my fancy,' said Gwyneth as she twisted away to brush her fiery mane before the looking glass.

Gwyneth made her way to the dining hall with the guard in tow. She never so much as looked at him and raised her nose whenever she had to look in his direction. The guard fell back and tried to shrink into the walls.

As they entered the huge hall, Gwyneth was reminded of the sheer size of her father's army. The hall was filled with officers of every rank and her thoughts ran to the thousands of men holed up in their tents out in the cold, beyond the walls. Up ahead her father sat at the main table with Morgan and a host of his best captains. Behind them, up on the wall, hung the standard of Voltar, the white stag staring straight at her.

Morgan's eyes caught hers and she noticed the sparkle of his braids with all their glass beads about his wizened face. A hush fell about the room as the men saw her father wave his hand for her to come over to his table and take a seat. The men rose from their chairs with a cacophony of wood on slate as she moved toward her seat beside the king.

'How are you my Lady,' asked Morgan as he rose to greet her with outstretched arms.

'I am well sir,' she replied as she gave him a hug, 'I would be better were I preparing myself for the important development that is afoot.' She glanced at her father with a wisp of a smile.

'Hah, you have not changed a bit young Gwyneth. You have certainly grown into a fine young woman but still giving your father grey hairs I see.' He smiled at the king who sighed in return.

'She would be the rebellious son I never had,' boomed the king, 'but I would have it no other way Morgan.' He too smiled his wry smile. 'Let us give thanks,' he continued.

Gwyneth noticed Tarrant at the table, half stooped out of his chair, his ear cocked in their direction, ever the spy she thought to herself. She sat down and looked the other way pretending not to notice him. Her father invited Tarrant to begin the rite of thanks for the meal. As usual, he stood up to begin the chant, raising his arms to make a big show of it just like a peacock, irritating her even more. As soon as it was over the men took their places at their tables and immediately started speaking all at once. There was a lot to discuss.

The conversation was of preparation for war and the many hardships they faced on the impending march to Caledon. Gwyneth looked about the room for her favourite captain, Goran Wilbur-axe. She heard the man's roaring laugh before she caught sight of his massive frame, arms gesticulating wildly as he relayed some story to the men at his table. By his side on the floor lay his faithful wolfhound, Bryn. Bryn was looking directly at her. His tongue hung loosely from the left side of his mouth with saliva steadily dripping in rhythm to his panting. She smiled at the big animal as he came over to have his head scratched.

VOLTAR MOBILISES

First light hinted at the window as Gwyneth awoke to the distant sound of her father's army mobilising. It had been three nights since Morgan's arrival and outside in the fog there was a lot of activity with commands shouted and the clatter of weaponry. Men mustered their horses but above all, she could hear the excited barking of the dogs. "Funny how they know what is happening," she thought. "Dogs baying for blood, what a sobering thought."

She dressed quickly and made her way down to the courtyard where her father and his captains were assembling. Her guard scurried after her trying to keep up. Her father was bidding farewell to Morgan who already sat upon his steed, his grey cloak flapping in the wind, catching his braids.

'Thank you my Liege,' Morgan was saying, 'I shall see you in the foothills near Caledon.'

'Ride with the Gods,' her father replied, 'we shall meet again my friend.'

'That we shall,' said Morgan as he waved at Gwyneth who appeared in the archway of the main entrance.

'Farewell fair maiden,' he cried across the courtyard as she waved in return. He reined in his steed, turned and made off into the fog, the sound of hooves on cold stone echoing in their ears.

'So the time has come my daughter,' the king said as he turned and walked towards her. 'You must keep the home fires burning and ensure the castle is intact for our return.'

'What choice do I have father?' she asked, tears welling up in her eyes.

'Now don't be like that my daughter, I must have you out of harm's way at a time like this. You refused to go to Druid's End with your mother and we now face mortal danger. Tarrant will be here to see to your needs and keep you in good health.'

'Keep me prisoner you mean,' she retorted, looking away to shield her disdain.

'Not so my love, would you have that I lose my daughter to the war that is about to befall us?' he asked.

'I want to be by your side father,' she implored. She hesitated a moment and then decided to acquiesce. 'Yet I understand and shall do your bidding.' She noticed Tarrant standing a few feet away, talking to a servant. She knew he was eavesdropping, always standing with his head tilted. Again, the one ear in the direction of the conversation he really meant to hear. The sight of him irked her inwardly. 'Father . . .' she wanted to tell him of her discovery the other night.

'Gwyneth, please do not cause me distress at a time like this,' her father said sadly. 'What is it my child?'

The look in his eyes begged a retreat. 'It is nothing. I shall miss you,' she cried, throwing her arms about him. This was not the appropriate time for discussing Tarrant. In any event, her father probably would not believe her now. It would all appear to be part of her grand design to have Tarrant denounced which, according to her father, she had been trying to do for nigh on a year. She wished he had never set foot in Voltar Regis.

' . . . and so shall I miss you too my dear one,' he replied, hugging her tightly.

Tarrant looked on in mock concern and she glared at him over her father's shoulder.

Through the fog, she heard a familiar bark and as she peered through the gloom, she could barely make out a form loping towards her. She stepped back from her father's embrace and looked in the direction of the gate. It was Bryn with his white coat appearing juxtaposed against the grey, dawn fog. His giant master appeared like a phantom behind him. Bryn ran up to Gwyneth, lifting onto his hind legs he planted two muddy paws on her shoulders and tried to lick her face. She squeezed him tightly and let him down gently. 'You naughty boy,' she cried.

'He's in love my Lady,' said Goran, with a broad smile.

'Ah, a fool then,' she said charmingly.

'There are no fools in love,' her father said wisely. 'Are your men ready?' He looked at Goran now, a veil of seriousness descending to shroud a half-smile.

'Yes my lord,' he answered. 'The additional provisions we were waiting for have all arrived and we are ready.'

'Good, give the signal for the march!'

Goran shouted a brisk order to his lieutenant standing just beyond the gate. The message carried down the hill and within moments, the sound of a clarion droned across the valley, echoing within the walls of Voltar Regis. The deep sound sent a cold shiver down Gwyneth's spine as she pulled her cloak about her chest. 'So it is time then,' she said emphatically.

'And so it is. A time of war,' her father replied quietly. 'Bring my horse,' he commanded a nearby attendant.

'Farewell my Princess,' Goran bid Gwyneth. 'May I leave with your blessing?'

'You have my blessing,' she said. 'Go with the Gods brave Goran.' She hugged him spontaneously, causing him to blush and pull away from her uncomfortably. He smiled and strode off towards his men as they stood in formation beneath their standards. They were just moving shadows beyond the huge gate, backlit by the many torches burning through the fog. Bryn yelped and ran after him, briefly looking over his shoulder at Gwyneth. Her father mounted his great steed and looked at her with sadness. He too smiled and then, in moments, was gone as fog closed in behind him and the scores of men out there.

Gwyneth looked around at the torches flickering against the wet walls of the fortress. She waited a few minutes, listening to the sound of her father's army beginning the long march to Caledon. A thousand images of war and adventure milled through her mind. She could hardly contain herself and decided to go back to her chamber, hoping the fog would lift for her to watch the activities from her window. As she entered the main building, she saw Tarrant scuttling off down a passage, with two browbeaten servants cowering at his heel. "Treacherous villain," she thought. "I wonder what he is up to."

She raced up to her room and had to stifle an uncontrollable urge to burst into laughter as she heard her guard huffing and puffing his way up the winding stairs behind her. "A bit of sport to quicken the blood," she thought. As she burst into her chambers, she slammed the door behind her. The key had been on the other side and fell to the ground with a tinkle and clatter. She quickly opened the door and with a deft hand retrieved the errant metal as the guard lumbered up the last steps. She locked herself inside and stood back watching the door as she heard him collapse into the chair. Turning she went to the window where the pale light of dawn stood blue against the panes, a cold intruder in the darkened room. Outside in the distance a thousand men were marching away down the valley, now visible as the fog began to dissipate. She stood transfixed by the spectacle until the sound of their feet thumping the earth became faint and she heard only her beating heart. A rooster crowed somewhere nearby, a sober reminder that this day had begun. "Dawn and I must away!" she thought.

It was time for her to make her escape and implement her plan to follow the army. She quickly went about gathering her provisions from under the bed and threw them into a leather bag drawing the strings together. She slung the bag over her shoulder. The previous day she had hidden her longbow and arrows along with her sword out in a wood at the edge of a field beyond the castle wall. It was on the way back from a hunting expedition to stock up for the provision wagons that she quietly broke away from the rest of the party as they watered their horses. To stop at the last well on the route back to Voltar Regis was a tradition and many villagers would gather around to take in the spectacle. She had hung back from the goings on and idle chatter to slip into the woods at the edge of the wheat field. She hid her weapons under the heather and tied one of the ribbons from her garment on a low hanging branch nearby.

She flung her servant's cloak around her and was about to make for the secret door in the cupboard when she heard voices on the other side of her bedroom door.

'Is she in there?' someone was asking.

'Yes sir, she's gone and locked herself inside!'

'Really, well that is good then. His Holiness Lord Tarrant has been very clear on watchin' that door and not letting her out of your sight. I'm not going to get a flogging over your foolishness, so you had better watch her good and don't go fallin' asleep you hear?'

'Yes sir, ooh I wouldn't do that, you can count on old Barnabas here sir,' was the reply from her tubby keeper.

'Good, then I will relieve your watch at midday,' and the voice drifted off together with the sound of shuffling feet, down the stairwell.

"That scheming bastard," she thought, "he is not going to make me a prisoner! Not as long as there is a sun in the sky by day or a moon by night!" With that, she quietly crept into the cupboard and once again made her way to the secret passage behind the wall. The thought did cross her mind that Tarrant might also know of this passage, just as he had known of the observation chamber behind the throne room. It did not matter now for should he cross her path in this tight space, she was determined that his heart would feel her steely dagger.

Gwyneth passed through the familiar corridors and halls like a ghost. There were only a few servants about, many having gone to witness the army's departure before starting their chores for the day. She decided not to go through the main courtyard but rather, to take the servants' route past the kitchens, and out to the stables. She made her way to her mount, a chestnut mare called Breeze, who stood alone and silent. Gwyneth heard a voice behind her.

'Who goes there?' It was one of the grooms on duty. She turned to face the young man who stood bravely before her at the entrance to the stables. 'I shall have at you!' he exclaimed, chest out and lantern held high.

'No need my man, Berwick isn't it?' she asked softly as she threw back her hood so that the yellow light caught her face and danced across her hair.

'Why yes it is I my Princess, apologies, I thought you were a thief,' he stuttered.

'Not a thief sir, just me going for a morning canter,' she smiled whimsically. 'You needn't go stirring up a hornet's nest now, and by the way, keep this our little secret won't you?' She winked at him and he blushed uncomfortably.

'Yes your highness, not a word,' he breathed.

'Now help me with my saddle and then go about your business and remember, not a word.'

He nodded furiously and then almost fell over himself trying to get the saddle and the horse ready. She abruptly thought better of blatantly striding out through the gates for all and sundry to witness. There may be prying eyes certain to be looking out for a possible runaway. Better to use another strategy.

'Actually, will you lead my horse out of the castle? Tell the guards that you are just taking her for her daily exercise. I will meet you just beyond the eastern wall.'

'Yes of course my Lady,' he said, taking on the demeanour of a man on a very important errand. He began leading the horse away.

'Thank you Berwick,' she smiled as he filed past her. Berwick smiled back and, once again, almost tripped over his own feet.

As soon as he was gone, Gwyneth made her way back past the kitchens and to the servants' entrance in the outer wall of the castle. From there it was just a skip across the yard, up a tower, over the bulwark and down her secret rope ladder to escape the bastions of Voltar Regis. It took her a few minutes to get to the entrance and as she did so, she tried the handle but the door had been locked.

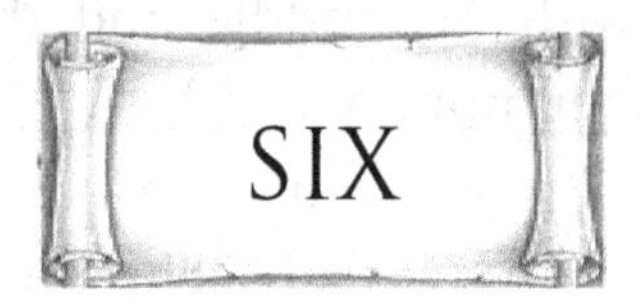

SIX

TRAITOR

Gwyneth's frustration was palpable; she huffed, bringing images of her father into her mind pointing a finger at her reprovingly. "Why is the key not in the door? It is normally here. It was here yesterday," she thought, as she had checked it herself just in case she needed this escape route. "That bastard has probably got the whole of Voltar Regis locked up good and tight like a wedge in a wall."

The servant's entrance to the castle was at the end of a short tunnel that ran from the kitchen. Gwyneth made her way back to the kitchens with her hood on and her head down. What was she to do? The kitchens were quiet, but would not be for long, she stopped to think. Just then Ruby entered via a far door and called out an urgent whisper, 'is that you m' Lady?'

'Yes, hush, not a word to anyone!'

'Are you looking for this?' Ruby held up a small copper key that reflected the morning light, a mischievous grin on her face.

'Ruby you little treasure,' rasped Gwyneth. 'How did you get your hands on this?' She reached out and grabbed the key.

'I heard Tarrant was locking things up good and tight to prevent you from escaping, so I locked up the servants' door before he got here and hid the key. When he asked after it, I told him it was lost and that we didn't use this door anymore. I knew you would probably be coming this way soon enough.'

'You clever little vixen,' Gwyneth said, with glee. 'No matter what happens you must not divulge our secret. Tarrant must not know that I have escaped beyond these walls.'

'Not to worry my Princess, I would never breathe a word to that mongrel dog,' Ruby spat in the direction of the stoves. 'Now make haste m' Lady before the kitchen comes to life. Many are on their way already with all the fuss around the king's departure.'

The Princess of Voltar Regis hugged her handmaiden and disappeared into the tunnel.

The sun had breached the horizon as Gwyneth made her way beyond the eastern wall through the scrub. Keeping within the tree line, she spied Berwick walking with Breeze. 'Here Berwick,' she whispered, 'over here.'

Berwick moved towards her and she waved for him to enter the woods. 'Thank you Berwick, now remember to keep this quiet, and go back via the servant's tunnel to the kitchens,' she handed him the key, 'and lock it up behind you and keep the key.'

'Yes m' Lady,' he said bowing his head.

'And stay among the trees, the guards must not see you return.'

'Yes of course m' Lady,' he handed Breeze over and took the key. 'Good luck me Lady,' he said as he waved and made his way back the way he had come.

Gwyneth led her mount in the other direction through the woods towards her hidden cache in the farmlands. The woods were cold and wisps of morning mist swirled around the large tree boles revealing roots at their bases like bulging noses and writhing limbs. The sun's wintery tendrils broke through the dark here and there and a nightingale sang a woeful tale somewhere nearby. She wondered why it had not left for warmer climes as many of the other forest dwelling birds already had.

It was a way to go before she neared her secret stash and she guided Breeze slowly, picking her way carefully through the thick wood. Her mount was ill at ease and Gwyneth sensed that Breeze was unhappy about something. She leant forward and stroked her mane, whispering reassuringly in her ear. Before the break at the edge of the woods, she heard a sound nearby. It was a cracking of twigs under foot and the rustle of something moving quickly at her flank in the brush.

Gwyneth dismounted in a flash and drew her dagger from beneath her cloak, throwing back her hood and freeing her ears so that she could better hear her attacker. All of a sudden, a large beast appeared out of the undergrowth and bolted towards her. In a split second, she raised her weapon to strike, but was met by the slobbering maw of Bryn.

'Why you sneaky boy,' she said, patting his head with one hand while returning the dagger to its scabbard with the other. 'What in damnation are you doing here you big oaf?'

'He accompanies his master,' said a familiar voice from somewhere in the trees. Goran stepped out of the shadows into a patch of dappled sunlight.

'Have you been following me?' asked Gwyneth indignantly.

'Well not following really my Lady, more like guarding you from a distance,' said Goran with a big grin.

'My father is behind this no doubt! Told you to stay behind and spy on me did he?'

'No not spy my Lady, but he knew you would probably try and do something rash, so he asked me to keep an eye on you while I . . .'

Gwyneth looked at him expectantly; 'well what?' she asked, as he shifted uncomfortably, 'and where is your horse?'

'My horse is tethered yonder but there are bigger fish to fry in Voltar Regis my Lady. I have been keeping my eye on the castle from afar for a few days now. Your father has been careful of late to inspect the movements of a certain person whom he has reason to believe is a real spy.'

'Oh!' she said, with interest. 'I bet I know who that would be, it's that malevolent old bastard Tarrant, isn't it?'

'Your father has had doubts about him for a while now and has received various reports from castle informants that he has been leaving the grounds in the middle of the night.'

'Where has he been going?'

'They don't know. Nobody has been able to follow him successfully. He manages to lose every tail.'

'Have you seen him this last night or this morning?' asked Gwyneth keenly.

'Not yet, but I am sure he will show his face soon. I have a spot up on a knoll not far from here which my scout is manning right now, let us go there, but we must be quick lest Tarrant eludes us.'

'I need to retrieve my weapons. I have hidden them near here.'

'No need my Princess; I have already collected them for you. You did not think that sly move of yours yesterday went unnoticed do you?' He beamed at her self-satisfyingly.

She said nothing and stared at him until the grin on his face waned.

'Uh, shall we?' he asked, turning from her and heading in the direction he had mentioned.

They made their way through the woods toward the north and the knoll Goran held. The sound of the horses' hooves thudding through the muddy undergrowth was all they heard, followed by a yelp from Bryn as they approached their destination. Gwyneth could see the rise of the small hill up ahead between the leafy evergreens and thought she saw some movement. Indeed, the young scout had stood up from his lookout position and leant his ear in their direction, lifting his hand to shield his eyes from the morning sun. 'Who goes there?' he called out.

'It is I, Goran,' he called back, 'any sign yet?'

'Nothing so far sir,' he answered, catching Bryn's head in his hands as the large hound pushed his nose into the young man's side.

'This is Mark,' Goran introduced his scout as they dismounted in the small clearing.

'M' Lady,' Mark bowed his head low and looked a little surprised and uncomfortable as Gwyneth smiled at him. She looked passed him and at the walls of Voltar Regis in the distance. Goran came and stood beside her and he too looked out at the vast buttresses of the castle as they cascaded away beyond the trees.

'A good vantage point for monitoring the comings and goings of the castle folk,' she said with interest, 'how long have you been watching?'

'A few days now; Mark here has been my eyes and ears.'

'So nothing yet?'

'Just the usual folk and of course the king's army early this morning,' Goran sighed longingly, 'that was quite an upheaval.'

'Who reported on Tarrant's little outings?' she asked.

'One of the tower guards said they had seen him go out about four nights ago.'

'Around the time Morgan was here?'

'Yes my Lady,' answered Goran.

'Very interesting!'

Goran noticed the realisation in her eyes and asked, 'what is it my Lady?'

'Well I know he has been poking his nose around in places it does not belong! I wonder who he is reporting to.'

'Yes this is what has vexed your father. We need to discover this secret and follow its trail to the convenor of this treason.'

'What if he tries to make an escape to the west or south from here?' asked Gwyneth.

'I have scouts on the other side of the castle too, but he was seen to be heading northwards before, and there are no gates or doors leading out to the west.'

They waited for the best part of an hour before Mark stood up and pointed to the edge of the wood. 'There,' he said, 'someone leaves on horseback!'

A dark figure in a hooded cape riding a black horse appeared beyond the tree line, cracking his whip as the animal bolted northwards. The party jumped into action and Bryn rushed around the horses barking excitedly.

'Quiet, not so much noise Bryn,' Goran hissed. Bryn's ears fell back in submission as he whimpered in frustration, still running circles around them.

The party made off in the direction of their quarry and beat a straight line through the woods. It was heavy going as they were not following any track and Gwyneth found herself fending off bough and branch as Breeze galloped after Goran's horse. Before long, they broke out of the forest and found themselves on the main road that skirted the northern walls. They followed the road beyond the castle precincts and over the first hill towards the farming villages. At the crest of the next hill, they stopped to survey the landscape to try to fathom the direction that the dark rider had taken.

'Where are you?' asked Goran under his breath as he surveyed the scene before them. The village lay in a small valley and beyond that, the crows swooped over the fallow wheat fields carpeting the landscape for miles in every direction. Copses of birch broke the undulating hills here and there and on the far horizon stood a row of fir trees. Snatches of the crows' hollow cries reached their ears but there was no other sign of life. 'Find him Bryn,' whispered Goran, urging his wolfhound on to the scent.

Bryn sniffed around the track, investigated a few weeds nearby, and then, with a triumphant bark, sprang off into a crazed lurching run ahead of them.

'He has him,' shouted Goran as they all darted after the big animal who seemed to be enjoying his mission immensely, barking over his shoulder as he sprinted forward. He led them past the village and up the next rise between the fields. Some farmers had surfaced from their morning toils on hearing the tumult and appeared at the edge of the village to witness the spectacle passing by.

Bryn led them between the fields and then veered off into the undergrowth near the woods to the northwest. The three riders passed into the woods and once again found themselves in a darkened place. They followed the wolfhound for a while but soon had to stop, as the growth ahead was too dense and thorny.

We will have to proceed on foot,' said Goran. He did not look very impressed. They could hear Bryn searching up ahead in the brush and then a growling snarl. 'Here boy,' he called as he realised his trusty companion had come upon something in the woods. 'Let us go around to the left as that way seems less unforgiving.'

They dismounted; leaving the horses hitched to a nearby birch and made for the area Goran had indicated. Mark went ahead, beating a track through the undergrowth before stopping abruptly and raising his hand. Gwyneth and Goran veered to his left and they all peered ahead through the trees to where an ancient ruin lay in a clearing. It was an old place of worship with large monoliths arranged in a circle and many other stones strewn across the ground. However, the sight of two figures communing at the centre of the site had them spellbound.

One of the figures was Tarrant and the other was something none of them had seen before. A tall, thin, dark form in a black, hooded cloak turned to look at them with a head that shocked them. An old, skeletal face peered out at them with yellow glowing eyes. The creature panicked as, in the same instant, Bryn broke into the clearing and tore straight towards it.

'No Bryn,' shouted Goran, 'get back!'

Tarrant spun around, his hand moving for his small crossbow. He levelled it in their direction. Everything happened in the blink of an eye from that moment on. They all ran forward as Bryn went into attack mode and lunged at the ominous apparition. Gwyneth raised her bow instinctively and let slip an arrow that found its mark in the heart of the black creature, which screeched in pain. Tarrant too had let loose a bolt from his weapon and it caught Mark in the stomach. As he fell to the ground clutching his midriff, Goran went to Mark's aid. Tarrant dashed into the woods behind him where his horse stood bucking in the turmoil. As Tarrant mounted his beast, it appeared to let out an awful sound and its whole form shook. With an ear-piercing scream that tore through the woods, the horse bolted bearing its rider at a speed like an animal possessed.

Gwyneth raced to the fallen form of the creature she had taken down. However, by the time she got to it, the form had withered and disintegrated before her eyes, the black cloak settling to the ground as a fine dark ash rose from the folds. She blinked, hardly believing her eyes and prodded the cloak with her foot.

'It has disappeared,' she said stunned, 'what dark power is this?'

'It is a Blackwraith,' answered Goran as Bryn went to him, his tail between his legs, obviously shaken by the whole ordeal.

'I have heard of them, I thought they were a myth. How bad is it?' she asked as she walked back to where Mark lay, his head cradled in Goran's arm. Goran met her eyes and shook his head.

'I'm sorry sir,' Mark stammered looking up at his captain, blood gurgling from his mouth.

'You are a brave man,' Goran whispered as he watched the light fade in the young scout's eyes. A moment later Goran screamed his condemnation towards the heavens, 'UNGODLY BASTARDS!'

The sombre comrades made their way back to the castle in silence, bearing Mark's lifeless form on his horse. They entered the confines of Voltar Regis where the hands and castle guard received them.

'Call for the undertaker,' Goran ordered dourly with an expression that gave the younger men the jitters. He looked at Gwyneth, 'we will have to send a bird to Ravencroft and a messenger after your father.'

'Yes,' granted Gwyneth, 'this changes things somewhat. Why don't we take the message to my father ourselves? This intelligence deserves priority and speed. What do you think he was up to and why was he in the company of that thing?'

'The Blackwraiths are the instruments of *Gordus Murdim*, the order of the Mask. We have all heard of the dark religion that has come to our shores from Mur. We thought we had seen the last of this demented bunch of fanatics. Tarrant is obviously a turncoat and a spy and must surely be in the Empress's service. She has been attempting to resurrect this evil cause for years. He could also be working for Dragar who is in bed with that witch.'

'Yes, after all, he did come to us as an emissary at Dragar's bidding did he not, as an advisor to my father in the affairs and common interests of Alton Savia and as a proponent of *our* faith? He has been up to no good for a while now and I never quite believed his fealty to the Earth-Goddess Mia. I have seen him spying on my father in conference with Morgan,' she said, angrily.

'Why did you not say something before my Lady?' he ventured.

'I tried to but the time was not right and then it was too late,' a look of guilt in her bright blue eyes.

'Morgan's undertaking could be in danger and possibly curtailed by this turn of events. Tarrant is gathering intelligence and is now off to share it with his collaborators. That horse is possessed by the creature and will no doubt be driven to death, since you destroyed the creature's body. We did not stand a chance really, I just wish I had killed Tarrant,' he said, as he looked to the floor.

'I have heard that is what they do, leave their bodies and take control of others.' Gwyneth shivered and made a sound that expressed her dislike. 'How do we eliminate them if destroying their bodies does not work?'

'We have to destroy the Mask. Only then will it finish them as they are driven by the Mask and its wearer,' he answered gravely; 'it will find another host, possibly human.'

'Let's write a message and send a raven immediately before it is too late my captain,' she said.

Goran nodded his agreement as they marched into the darkened halls of the castle.

A DARKENING IN KARN

Karn was a dangerous city that lay to the east of Caledon on the northern coastal perimeter of the Kingdom of Arillon. It was not a beautiful city by any means and people often referred to it as the ugly sister to Caledon further up the Aral River. Where Caledon sported lofty golden spires, Karn was dark and sombre. Grey stone buildings and many stores and warehouses lined both sides of the river mouth as it opened to the sea. Karn was a trading city with a large busy port, which hosted many foreign ships that plied their trade up and down the Murian Strait. It was commonplace to see the tall, silver masts and billowing purple sails of the Kalvari from the Western Isles and more recently the foreign looking, squat, black schooners of Mur in the harbour. Seeing Murian ships would have been unheard of a year ago but now, with the new treaty between the king and the empress from across the water, many past taboos had been broken. Not many people were happy with the new order, apart from the wealthy merchants who stood to gain from the influx of exotic goods and of course, the king's tax collectors. Many people felt that the northern barbarians were invading Arillon and there were often spats in the street, brawls in the local taverns and a general ambiance of xenophobia.

Jeb was one of the few who actually enjoyed getting mixed up in the milieu. His little band of brothers was doing well under the stewardship of Kruger, the head of the hoodlums. They were a ragtag bunch of street urchins, rough and tumble, all orphans and outcasts. Pickings, in the past months, had been quite slim for their tastes, especially for the smuggling fraternity. The Kalvari were quite a cunning bunch and all but excluded the local criminality. Now things were looking up thanks to the more gregarious Murians. They were slave traders, womanisers, and drunkards and got their hands dirty any way they could.

Today he was meeting Kruger in their den. Well he liked to think of it as their den, it was really a sailor's tavern tucked away in the docklands near the warehouses, where they had commandeered a little table in a back corner. It was their haunt of choice. They actually had a few meeting places scattered around Karn, but this one was always warm and friendly due to their relationship with the owner. Maggot, as they affectionately knew him, took Kruger in as a young lad, and found him quite useful for running illegal errands. His insalubrious and enterprising character had rubbed off on Kruger over the years and had inspired him to enlist his own little band of vagabonds. "Up scaling," he liked to call it. They were always on the lookout for more members and in past weeks had been on a drive to attract even more young recruits. Jeb was one of the first and in a way felt a little threatened by this new undertaking. He thought of the original five gang members as the founding fathers. There was Kruger and himself, Buttons who came next in the pecking order, then little Johnny and most recently Sara who was the youngest and the only girl on the team.

Maggot had urged Kruger to round up at least five more children from the poor districts of Karn and bring them to his establishment. He had a "master plan" that needed a large gang and apparently, this was going to be the mother lode. He remembered the look in the fat, swarthy, old man's eye as he wrung his hands in anticipation of the fortune they would win for him.

It was a cold day with a sky that hung heavy overhead and a wind that whistled through the streets making women clutch at their bosoms and men drive their hands ever deeper into their pockets. Jeb felt the cold keenly and longed for a warm coat. "Maybe a thick fur from Caledon," he thought to himself as he edged his way through the low-rise buildings to the "*Mermaid Inn.*" He was definitely going to buy one with his share of the loot. He tried to imagine what this new plan might entail and hoped that it involved robbing some wealthy area of the city. He thought that he might garner some additional belongings along the way. The tinkle and glitter of fine jewellery held a special place in his heart. He saw the inn up ahead and remembered how hungry he was, it being midday. He hoped Maggot had something warm for them to eat as he opened the creaking, pockmarked door and entered the noisy inn.

In the hearth, a fire roared and the place smelled of the usual mead mixed with a bouquet of red wine, sweaty bodies and damp straw underfoot. The room was packed, as usual, and the clamour of voices rose above the crackling logs. Sailors sat with voluptuously breasted tarts on their laps. Someone was playing a local rendition of an old ditty on a fiddle and people sang and clapped in merry unison. He made his way to the back of the room and through a low arch to their usual table.

There he saw a veritable crowd huddled in around Kruger who stood out far above the rest.

'Allo son!' Kruger beckoned Jeb into his inner sanctum. 'Where you been son?'

'Here and there,' he replied with a wink.

'Well we're all here now. Let me introduce you to our new little blighters.' He waved his hand in a swashbuckling arc as he presented five new young sets of wide eyes that stared on expectantly. 'Here we 'ave Brian, Gratin, Mug, Charlie and . . . ?'

'Bo,' said a small waif kneeling on the floor with his tiny arms folded in front of him on the table.

'Yes of course. Bo,' he said with a wily smile.

'All new friends,' said Sara grinning, one of her upper front teeth missing.

'Where's your tooth?' asked Jeb.

'It fell out!' She giggled.

'I'm hungry,' said Buttons.

'Me too,' echoed six timid voices.

Just then, Maggot walked up and banged a steaming pot of garlic mussels onto the middle of the table along with a stack of bowls. 'Well I'm just in time then, ain't I?' he said. The group jumped forward all grabbing at the bowls in frenzy. 'Now, now,' he said, 'there is enough for everyone. I'll be back with some bread.'

'I'll serve it up,' said Kruger sternly, putting them all in their place. They all settled back and eagerly pushed each of their bowls forward, nearer to the pot. Kruger dished up two ladles full to each bowl as Maggot came back with hunks of bread.

'My own recipe,' Maggot said, beaming.

'It's lovely,' slurped Brian and a bunch of feeding heads nodded agreement, dirt-stained hands grabbing bread.

'Well I'm glad you all like it,' said Maggot wringing his hands, 'there's more where that came from. But now it's time to talk business.'

'Yes,' said Kruger, 'we have a plan that will make us all rich!'

'Rich,' echoed Maggot, 'beyond your wildest dreams.'

'What is it?' asked Jeb, excitedly. His mind raced with ideas of grandeur.

It was an elaborate plan and Maggot went on to explain how it was all to go ahead and how each person had a very important part to play. It involved an unsavoury bunch of Murian smugglers who were expecting delivery of four dozen boxes of the much sought after, inordinately expensive and very beautiful indigo Kalvari silks from Ishtar, hence the need for the large team. The window of opportunity was small and the whole operation had to work to precision. Kruger had drawn up a plan with stations for everyone and they all had cues to follow. It was a long-winded plan and Kruger relished his position as the main protagonist in this plot as he assigned the various jobs. He unfurled an old, stained map and placed it before them, moving bowls out of the way, as he did so. It was to be a dangerous mission as the Murians were stealing from the Kalvari and any number of things could go wrong. The Murian gang did not want to be identified and would be pulling the strings from a distance. They would only be meeting one Murian contact on the dock while more Murians would be ready to receive the goods on their barge. The barge would then sail on to a merchant in Caledon.

'So as you can see there is a lot to do,' said Maggot.

'A lot to do,' repeated the younger villain, parrot fashion. 'Now, does everyone know what they are doing?'

'Yes, yes,' were the answers.

'So Kruger will be waiting here with the wagon,' Maggot pointed to an "x" on the map with a pudgy, brown finger, 'and you all have to get there at the same time so that he can get you over to the barge here,' another "x."

They all nodded vigorously and then Jeb piped up, 'what's in it for us?'

'Ah yes, the payment,' said Maggot sardonically, 'well each of you will be getting TEN silver coins!'

This was a lot of money and their eyes widened collectively. Jeb had only ever owned one silver coin before and almost could not believe it. The only reason he had acquired the coin was that it was in the purse of a wealthy lord he had pick-pocketed in the outer reaches of the city. He would be lucky to get even a single copper coin these days. This was a marvellous turn of events and he could definitely buy his fur coat now. He smiled in anticipation.

'So we will all meet here tomorrow at sunset,' Kruger indicated the rendezvous point on the map, 'and remember to wear these black tunics.' He deposited a hessian bag on the table and began distributing the garments that Maggot had acquired from his Murian counterparts. 'There is a warm room upstairs for you tonight and tomorrow we will rehearse our plan.'

After eating their fill and talking for hours about the excitement that lay ahead, the children finally made their way up to the beds that Maggot had so kindly provided for them. Upstairs, once they were all warmly tucked in, they shared the plans they had in mind for the wealth they were about to acquire.

They spent the following day in the *Mermaid Inn* gathered around the table, rehearsing the planned course of events. Maggot kept them well fed and the younger ones could not believe their luck, most of them not knowing what it was like to have three square meals in one day. There were loaves of bread, cinnamon buns with currants, a great salty broth and sweet orange juice to finish it all off. They had all had a jolly good rest the night before, sleeping two to a bed with the three smallest children sharing a bunk. The day wore on with Kruger going over everyone's instructions repeatedly. He then made each of the children recite their part, like a hard taskmaster. They all had to be down at the wharf just after sunset and wait in one of the small warehouses at the third jetty, where a Murian by the name of Drax would meet them. They then had to move the cart he would provide over to another building, where the cargo was stored, and load it up. Kruger was to keep the night watch distracted. They would then run the cart all the way to the last jetty and up a ramp onto the barge where they were to unload it into the hold.

The sunlight dwindled swiftly over the darkened horizon as, without notice, a squall came in off the Murian Strait. As it turned out this would probably aid them in their endeavour, as there would not be many people around the docks and the watch would be well ensconced in their warm office. They were wearing the black smuggler's attire, which proved quite rough with everyone pulling at the fabric and rubbing at their itching skin. Jeb thought they looked like a small dark army.

'Well it's time,' said Kruger in a solemn tone.

'Good luck my lovelies,' said Maggot, grinning from ear to ear as he ushered them out the back of the inn, into the freezing rain that fell heavily at an angle, drenching them within seconds.

Kruger led them down towards the water's edge in single file. Sara slipped on the wet cobbles and Jeb had to help her up more than once. They made their way to the rendezvous point where the cart was waiting. On arrival, fear gripped them when they saw the massive Drax waiting for them. He was over six feet tall with dark, gleaming muscles and gold earrings.

His attire was typically Murian with brightly coloured, striped, flowing robes and a dark, cloth headdress wrapped around his large head with a piece hanging down his back, almost like a ponytail.

'Here,' he barked, rolling his "r," as he herded them into a shed. There they found the cart that was covered in a large canvas. They waited while Kruger ran along the wharf to find and distract the watch, if needed, and stand as lookout. 'Let us go now,' Drax hissed.

'Come on then,' coaxed Jeb as they put their backs into rolling the two-wheeled vehicle out into the night once Kruger gave the signal. He had perfected a seagull's call and they heard the three consecutive little screeches just above the noisy lanyards and cleats slamming against the many masts around them. The three smallest members, Sara, Bo, and Buttons, hid under the tarpaulin so as not to hinder the subsequent goings on.

Drax and the children reached the appointed store. There was nobody around. A lantern shone through the odd window but to all intents and purposes, the coast was clear. Drax broke the locks with a large crowbar and ushered them in, closing the doors behind them. They were quick as mice as they loaded the boxes onto the cart before, once again, covering the whole lot with the canvas tarpaulin. Jeb was to go out and signal Kruger that they had completed the first part of the task. He would then confirm that it was safe to move on.

'Right, we go,' said Drax and once again, they were fighting the driving rain with their cargo. This time it was heavy going with the extra weight. They rushed down the wharf, the wooden wheels clamouring across the uneven stones, and then onto the jetty. Before long, the barge loomed black in front of them and the ramp that had been set in place for their arrival came into view. Lanterns appeared above them and they could hear the strong Murian accents of the sailors.

'Here, here,' the Murians called.

In the rush Drax had to help the children with the last drive onto the deck, 'quickly we must offload into here,' he directed.

'Let's move! Fast, fast,' shouted the Murians.

Once again, they formed their line from the cart and down a ladder unloading the contents into the hold. It did not take them long at all; the planning paid off, as everyone knew exactly what to do.

'Good, very good,' said Drax once they had finished and then, simply and without warning drew his curved scimitar and indicated for the children still above deck to move towards the hold doors.

'What's happening,' implored Jeb, the look of surprise on his white face clearly visible in the half-light. Someone else screamed and two of the children tried to escape, scattering across the deck in frenzy, but it was to no avail. Jeb instinctively made a dash for the side, in the hopes of tumbling overboard and swimming to safety. He fell to his knees and darted between Drax's legs, confusing the massive Murian who grunted in frustration as he tried to catch his quarry.

Jeb made it to the edge and in a second he had mounted the rail when, to his horror, a large hand grabbed him by the ankle. He was dangling in mid air above the water and from his upside down position; he saw a glint of gold and a smirk in the darkness.

The Murians rounded them up, like frightened little goats, throwing them headlong down into the dark hold. They crashed into Bo and Buttons, falling over each other as they all tumbled down the ladder. The sailors retracted the ladder and closed the heavy doors, shutting them in as the sound of chains rattling through the fastening rings above them left them in darkness.

EIGHT

THE CATACOMBS

Jeb could not believe what had happened. He sat on a pile of rope feeling as if all hope was lost. A deep sadness welled up in him, nearly bringing him to tears. He felt like he would burst out crying like a babe. However, he knew that he had to be strong for the others, some of whom had been sobbing incessantly for hours. They were huddled against him like a litter of puppies around their mother. Sara and Bo did not let go of his legs all night. The barge had left the dock shortly after they had been imprisoned and Jeb was preoccupied with thinking about whether Kruger and Maggot knew about his fate. He thought about where the Murians were taking them and after about half an hour he realised they were heading up river. Their passage was smooth and they had not encountered the rough open sea. "Good," he thought, "at least they are not taking us to Mur!" Maybe they were going to Smithfield,

Laurel, or maybe even one of the smaller towns upstream; or maybe they were going all the way up to Caledon.

'What is to become of us?' asked Brian.

'Well we are not heading out to sea,' he answered.

'How can you tell?' asked Bo.

'Well the water is quite calm.' Gratin offered his wisdom now.

'Yes that is true,' Jeb concurred, 'they are taking us upriver. I am guessing to a workhouse in one of the larger towns, or it may be that they are taking us all the way to Caledon.'

'Caledon,' repeated Buttons with awe, 'I always wanted to go there.'

Some light filtered through the grate in the hold doors from the swinging hurricane lamp above. Jeb could see the wonderment in the young eyes around him, but also the abject fear. He felt a pang of guilt for having been jealous of the newcomers joining the family.

It suddenly dawned on him that this whole affair might have been a plot hatched by Maggot. From the sudden need to recruit more members and the way he had been behaving lately, to the look on his face when they left the inn. He felt responsible for the others now and said pragmatically, 'well there is not much we can do right now so let us try and get some sleep.'

They clung together, seeking warmth from the proximity of each other's bodies and shivering through the night in the cold, damp innards of the barge as it made its way swiftly to its unknown destination. Surely, Maggot and Kruger had not had a hand in this chain of awful events; after all, he had been entrenched with them for over six months now. It just could not be! Where were the Murians taking them to and to what end? Maybe they were taking them to Caledon to conscript them into the king's new army. Rumours of the army abducting young men had circulated recently, other men disappeared altogether, but he and his cohorts were all children and he had never heard of children going missing or being press ganged into the ranks of the military. It did not make any sense, he pondered on these, and other strange and fanciful possibilities well into the night until he finally fell into a fitful and uncomfortable sleep.

The next day was just as wet and cold and the children were so thirsty that they were sucking at the trickles of fresh rainwater that ran down the inside of the bulkheads. Eventually Jeb could not take it anymore and screamed up through the grate. 'Hey there, we are hungry and thirsty! Do you want us to die before we get to our destination?'

There was no answer and yet he could hear men above moving around, going about the business of sailing the vessel. He screamed even louder a few more times until he thought he would become hoarse and eventually a head appeared above them.

'What do you want, waif?' the silhouette screamed.

'We need water and sustenance sir,' he pleaded, changing his tone to one of supplication. There was a hullabaloo of sorts as the Murian consorted with someone else. A few minutes later, someone removed the heavy chain from the doors above and opened them to let down a bucket of water and a bag of stale bread. 'Thank you sir,' he hollered as the great hold doors slammed shut.

The hungry group crowded around Jeb as he divvied the small, hard loaves up and allowed each one to drink from the bucket. He had to tell them not to have too much water, as they needed to save some for later. The day rolled on and they spoke about what had happened and what might happen until very late in the day. As the sun appeared to set outside, their captors filled their bucket again and this time dropped down a bag of overripe fruit. None of the children said anything as they ate the food provided for them. Jeb spent the entire evening thinking of escape. At this stage, escape was futile as the drop from the hold door was at least seven feet. He would have a better chance of figuring out the possibilities once they arrived at wherever it was they were going.

The rest of their voyage was much the same. It was cold, wet, and uncomfortable with rats scuttling around and nibbling at their extremities. It was a constant battle with the rats on the second night. Jeb thought of his mother, which he seldom did, as it made him feel sad. The plague had taken her a few years before when he was only four years old but he remembered her kind eyes and soft voice and how she used to sing him to sleep with lullabies when he was unsettled. He missed her terribly now. Hers was the only true kindness he had known in his short life. He longed for the safety of her arms yet knew that this could never be.

The next day they received water, old bread and more overripe fruit causing them all to feel rather ill. Jeb was certain the horror would never end but eventually, on the afternoon of the third day; they could feel the boat scrape up against a mooring. Men above were making ready for the landing.

The sun made its debut in a painted blue sky welcoming the weary and very stiff party of nine. Their eyes hurt from the sudden bright light. They were ushered onto the deck like a herd of sheep by four large, armed, brazen looking Murians and Drax. They were chained together with manacles one to another like a line of convicts, before being forced towards a waiting horse-drawn wagon. Jeb's eyes adapted quickly and it did not take him very long to figure out that they were in Caledon. The harbour city rose behind the docks in a kaleidoscope of rooftops, all the way up to the colossal outer walls of the palace citadel known as Calavaria. This soared above all else with a plethora of towers and turrets all fighting for pre-eminence against the sky. The green, gold and white colours of Arillon flew from every parapet and spire. The walls of the entire place shone golden and amber as the winter sun reflected off the yellow stone. This was a glorious monument built to pay homage to the Kings of Alton Savia.

However, there was not much time to take in the spectacle as the Murians forced them into the wagon and locked it up. They covered the small windows on either side with cloth to hide the interior of the wagon from prying eyes. With the crack of a whip, they began to move along the wharf and onto the cobbled streets. They could hear the clattering hooves above a cacophony of city sounds and voices as they travelled through the docklands to the inner reaches of the capital. As they were moving uphill, Jeb could tell that they were heading towards the dreaded Calavaria, which occupied the highest point of the sprawling city of Caledon. The children whispered amongst themselves not knowing what to expect and Jeb had to reassure the younger ones who shed more tears of fear.

After an hour, the wagon rambled to a halt and the rear door was flung open to reveal the dark maw of a cave lit by torches high up on the moss-green stone walls.

'Where are we?' asked Jeb.

'You shall see,' grunted Drax, giving him a wallop on the back. Jeb lost his breath and stumbled to the ground nearly taking Brian down with him. They entered the cave and their captors forced them down a winding tunnel into the depths of the earth beneath the city. It was stifling and warm. Torches lit the way at intervals high on undulating walls before finally ending in a large cavern. The cave was enormous with stalactites protruding from the darkness. These protrusions from above glowed with an inner luminosity that cast an eerie, green light over a dark, reflective subterranean lake. Water dripped into the lake sending ripples in every direction and the sound echoed through the cave like some strange underground choral arrangement. This strange world fascinated the children.

'In here,' barked Drax as he pointed into a deep alcove enclosed by iron girders. They had no choice but to follow his orders and found themselves locked in a prison of sorts, a small cave tapering back a few metres. The children grasped the iron grille and stared out at the baffling scene. Once the Murians had left, they were on their own again.

'Bloody hell,' said Bo, 'what is this place?'

'It's scary,' said Sara, rattling her chain.

'It smells terrible in here,' said Buttons, wrinkling his nose.

'Yes, like dead things,' said Gratin, his face a picture of terror. He moved closer to Jeb looking for comfort.

'I don't like it either,' whined Sara, following Gratin's lead and sidling in on the other side of Jeb.

'What is happening, are we slaves?' asked Johnny.

'I think we are,' said Charlie, 'but where in Mia's name are we?'

'I think we are beneath Calavaria,' said Jeb.

'Calavaria,' repeated Charlie with disbelief, 'but they don't take slaves here do they?'

'Looks like they do now,' answered Jeb miserably. The children went on chattering before they gradually nodded off, one by one. Jeb tried to stay awake but he too soon succumbed and his head dropped to his chest as he leaned back against the rear cell wall.

They jolted awake to the sound of someone unlocking the gate and the light of a torch as it bobbed above their heads. Two guards wearing the colours of Arillon approached their cell. Jeb could clearly see the golden lion with the green and white background on their breastplates. The rest of the uniform was brown leather with a black cape. They carried swords and did not say anything as they arrived to unlock the chains from two of the children. They guided Brian and Johnny out of the prison and away.

'Where are we going? I don't want to!' pleaded Johnny, 'No, no!' His screams echoed through the caves until they trailed off. They dragged him and Brian down one of the winding tunnels that branched off from the main cavern.

Jeb noticed many smaller caves and tunnels leading in every direction, which he had not really noticed before. The whole place was like one gigantic subterranean labyrinth. In places, he was sure he could see faces peering out of the shadows at them. He mulled on this for a while before it dawned on him; they were skulls. They were in the Catacombs of Calavaria. All his life he had heard the scary stories about this place, particularly told on cold dark nights around the fire. Arillon's dead of ages past surrounded them!

'Where are they taking them?' asked Sara with a look of dread in her eyes.

'I don't know little one,' he answered.

'I'm hungry!' Gratin spoke with bulging eyes.

'Maybe we will get fed when they take us,' said Bo.

It was many long hours later before the guards were back to take another two children and then another until there were only Sara, Buttons and Jeb remaining. They clung to each other in fear awaiting their fate. Hours later, they heard men approaching and saw the light of their torches weaving through the tunnels. The guards arrived and dragged the three little captives from their cell not bothering to unchain them, as they were the last. The others had been unlocked from the main group but still left bound together in pairs as the guards marched them off. The sword-bearers forced the children to take a route around the side of the lake. For a fleeting moment,

Jeb thought he saw something moving beneath the water. He blinked twice and was sure he had seen something long and scaly like a large fish but decided it was the light playing tricks on him. Their captors herded them through an opening and into a long tunnel.

'Look there,' whispered Sara as she pointed out a mound of human skulls stacked and embedded in the wall of a nearby recess.

'Skeletons,' whispered Buttons, 'hope we don't end up like that.'

One of the guards laughed and Jeb did not like the sound of it one single bit.

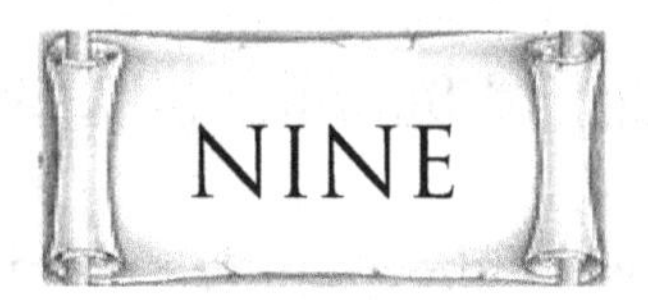

NINE

A SERVANT OF ARILLON

The tunnel continued steeply uphill, eventually leading the guards and their prisoners to a small, heavy, studded door. One of the guards produced a large key that hung from his waist and forced it into the keyhole. He grappled with the lock for a few moments until eventually, the mechanism turned with a loud click. Beyond the door, they found a flight of grey, stone stairs that continued into the darkness above them. They ascended a few hundred steps and passed through another door and, on passing through yet another, they realised they were within the confines of the palace dungeons. There were gated cells, oubliettes, and large metal cages suspended on heavy chains from the stone arches above. The captive trio were sickened to discover that one of the cages contained their friends, Brian and Johnny. They waved at them but the two boys did not seem to notice them at all and stared ahead vacantly with large dull eyes.

'What's wrong with them?' asked Sara as the corners of her little mouth pushed down.

'I don't know,' said Jeb, 'but don't look at them.'

'I want to go back to Karn,' whimpered Buttons.

The guards took the children up another short flight of stairs into a narrow corridor with doors on either side and then flung them through one of the doors into a small room. They slammed the door shut and locked the children inside. There was straw on the floor and a bucket of water in the corner from which the trio tried to drink as much as they possibly could. They scooped handfuls at a time until they had finally had their fill. Jeb fell back wiping his mouth and catching his breath before noticing, for the first time, that there was a tiny, narrow window high up in the wall. He could see stars twinkling in the night sky outside and felt a wisp of fresh, cool air on his cheeks. Strangely, he felt the slightest glimmer of hope, the first since leaving Karn, as the connection to the world outside made him feel free. The three children lay together on the straw and slept until the light of early morning eked its way into their small world.

'Up, up you lot!' A voice called through a hole in the door. The door was unlocked and opened to expose a stout, hardy looking woman. She wore the uniform of a scullery maid and her dark hair was pulled back in a tight knot to reveal a hardened face and hawkish eyes. 'Now don't be giving me any trouble young 'uns,' she said, 'because there is nowhere to run and you will pay dearly for any mischief! Now follow me.'

They did her bidding and followed her out of the room and along the passage through another door. She led them through a maze of tunnels and doors until they finally arrived at a large kitchen. A guard stood stony silent in a corner and stared at them blankly as they entered. The children could not believe their eyes. There was a table laden with all kinds of food in various stages of preparation. Jeb felt his mouth water as he gaped at the feast before them. They were seated on a long oak bench, side by side, as she set three bowls before them.

'Some nourishment for hungry souls,' she said, smiling as she filled their bowls with a meaty broth.

'For us?' asked Sara, incredulously.

'Yes me darlin's, you must be famished, poor things.'

'We are Miss,' answered Jeb, 'thank you Miss.'

They wolfed down the food and gratefully accepted the bread she offered.

'My name is Oonagh,' she said, emphatically.

'Thank you Oonagh,' they chorused with mouths full.

She sat and watched them as they ate and then offered them water in pewter mugs. There was silence as they finished their meal. Eventually, once they sat licking their fingers, Jeb asked, 'why are we here Oonagh?'

'Ah, I couldn't tell you my dears,' she said, 'I am not privy to the policy and goings on of this court. All I know is I am to have you fed and cleaned up and delivered to the chambers of his Lordship, the Prelate of Arillon.'

'Who is that?' asked Buttons.

'Too many questions for your station young man,' she answered and ushered them into an adjoining room where she unlocked their chains and freed their bruised and scratched ankles. Oonagh bathed them in a large tub of fragrant, hot water. None of them had ever had a bath before and found the whole experience rather off-putting yet quite pleasant at the same time. She gave them plain, grey tunics to wear, tied with a plaited, silver chord. The cloth was of a good quality and they all looked at each other in disbelief once the grime and sweat washed off their bodies and these seemingly stately garments replaced their rags.

'And now you must go with him,' she pointed towards the guard who had stood watching the whole affair in silence.

'This way,' he said, leading them out of the kitchens.

The freshly scrubbed trio followed him out and into a large colonnade that opened onto a vast hall. There were guards everywhere and Jeb thought better of his urge to run. Escape was not going to be possible right now, he imagined. The palace was vast and more beautiful than any building he had ever seen. The floors were made of white marble and there were enormous marble pillars that rose to a painted, vaulted ceiling. Between the pillars stood large statues of kings and queens, covered in gold leaf. He was sure he could see precious stones embedded in their crowns and sceptres. Behind these were large standards depicting green fields and white skies and the emblazoned golden lion of Arillon. To Jeb the morning sun shining down through the stained glass windows high above them looked like spears of light illuminating everything in dappled shades of pink, mauve, and blue. The sight took his breath away as he and his fellow prisoners scuttled after the guard in their bare feet.

Beyond the hall, the guard led them up a winding staircase and finally into a large room clearly set up as an audience parlour. At one end there was a large, ornate chair covered in red velvet and set upon a dais with a red curtain as a backdrop. In front of this, an arrangement of benches stood in rows. There were four guards standing to attention with their backs to the walls, holding long pikes.

'Sit here and wait,' bade their escort. He left the room and the doors closed quietly behind him. The children sat in silence, staring from one to another and around the room. Finally, there was some movement from behind the curtain. A thin man appeared. To Jeb he looked like a scarecrow he had seen in a cornfield once but this one was bald with a large hook for a nose and a face that made him cringe in fear. A small man followed the scarecrow and took his place beside him like some kind of pet.

'His eminence, Lord Tarrant,' sprouted the sidekick with a flourish. He looked at the children and blinked, 'you must bow!'

The children all stood up at once and bowed awkwardly.

'Be seated,' he said. They sat down, fidgeting uneasily.

'You are now wards of this court,' said the Lord Tarrant in a high, fluting voice that echoed around the room. 'Do you know where you are?'

The children nodded as he stared at them, expressionless.

'Well where are you?' he asked. His voice was haughty and condescending.

'Calavaria m' lord,' answered Jeb, sheepishly.

'That is correct,' he said, tersely, 'Calavaria. And do you know who rules in Calavaria?'

'King Dragar of Arillon,' answered Jeb.

'That is correct! Why you are a clever one, are you not?' he sneered.

'Yes sir . . . I mean no sir,' said Jeb.

He glared down his nose at Jeb. 'Do you know me boy?' he asked with malice.

'No sir,' answered Jeb.

'Well let me inform you then. I am your new master and from now on you will answer only to me and do as I bid you, is that clear?'

They all nodded vigorously.

'You have been specially selected to work in this court. The staff will feed, clothe, and house you at my discretion. You are apprentices,' he stated, factually. 'You are very lucky,' he continued, 'do you understand?'

'Yes sir,' they answered.

'Take those two younger ones with the others to the temple workhouse and prepare them for the ritual, Shram,' he said, pointing at Sara and Buttons. 'I will take care of this one myself.' Tarrant clearly meant Jeb who suddenly felt a cold hand grip his stomach. 'Follow me boy,' he beckoned Jeb.

Shram ushered the others out of the room and Jeb followed Tarrant behind the curtain, a guard on his tail. He looked over his shoulder to see Buttons and Sara looking over theirs with pained expressions on their young faces. He so dearly wanted to go over and give them both a reassuring hug but feared there might be some terrible form of retribution at the hands of this awful man. Sara waved and he did the same.

Beyond the curtain he was led into another small chamber and then along a number of passages. Before long, they were in a small room that looked like an apothecary, with all kinds of bottles and vials arranged on shelves and tables.

'Sit here,' said Tarrant, motioning towards a chair. Jeb did not argue and hastened to comply. 'You are a strong willed, young man and will be my personal little helper.' He opened a small, ornate box that was on the table and produced a tiny talisman of black stone set in a metal casing. The talisman hung suspended on a leather chord and Lord Tarrant placed it over Jeb's head so that the stone lay just below his throat. 'This gift will help keep your mind in focus,' he said slowly, as his long fingers retracted and his eyes bore into Jeb.

The room faded around Jeb as if a grey mist had risen to shroud everything and he felt as if he were sinking below water. He was sick to his stomach and all he could register was Tarrant's large eyes and soothing voice.

'Your mind is cleared of everything except my voice,' Tarrant droned. Jeb felt as if the talisman was weighing him down while Tarrant's voice seemed to be coming at him from a distance. 'Yes, that will do very nicely I think.'

Jeb thought he was dreaming but could not be sure. Nothing around him appeared real anymore and now he became aware that the voice he was hearing was no longer an external thing, but rather an internal experience. The voice was in his head and it was asking him to do something. What was it saying? It was a strange language he did not know or understand. Yet he could grasp its meaning. It was the voice of the master. This was the voice of *his* master. Yes, that was it, he was to walk over to the window and look out. The master wanted him to go and have a look at what was happening outside and report his findings. Jeb could not help himself and could feel his legs moving, taking him in the direction of the window. He was aware that he had no control. What was happening to him? He could not fight it; he had to yield. He had to follow the instruction. At the window, he looked out at the city around him. A voice started coming out of him, it was his own voice, 'I see buildings and flags and people and trees.'

The master was pleased and Jeb's head started to clear. The master's voice receded. The world became whole again, he was not dreaming, no he was Jeb, here in the room. He looked around, trying to focus on something he could identify with, something solid and real to make the feeling go away. He looked down at his feet; his toes, they were his toes.

'Very good,' said Tarrant, 'you will do very well young man.'

'What happened?' he asked, 'where am I?'

'You are in a safe place. Everything will be fine now.'

'I am in a safe place,' he repeated.

'Yes, very safe. It is time for you to go to your quarters and meet your new friends. Shram, your new instructor will school you in the laws of Arillon and the ways of Calavaria. You are in my service now as a servant to the throne of Arillon.'

'I am a servant to the throne of Arillon,' he repeated.

A guard collected him and led him through many corridors and down many stairs to the worker's rooms next to the stables. There were other boys there too, all about the same age as he was. They too wore the grey tunics of the court and he noticed that they also had a talisman about their necks, just like his.

Jeb did not like the feel of this stone as it weighed him down. He reached for it to rip it off and free himself of this burden but he could not. It was too heavy and he did not have the strength. Why was it so heavy? It was meant to be there. It was meant to be a part of him. His desire to rid himself of the worrying necklace started to fade and he soon no longer thought of it. Instead, he began to think about the boys he had just met. They all belonged together in the service of Calavaria. He was now in the service of his new master, Lord Tarrant.

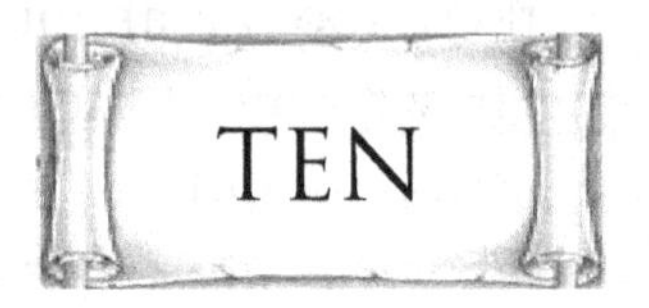

TEN

A PERILOUS JOURNEY

The track meandered around the mountain like a dry, sandy river, pushing ever upwards. On both sides, dense pine forest surrounded the riders. The trees rushed by as Dorian and his escort rode with the wind at their backs. The dark tree trunks looked like so many soldiers jostling for attention beneath a thick roof of green. The forest was deathly quiet apart from the sound of their horses' hooves drumming the dirt in a rhythmic tempo.

Dorian reflected upon the strange events that had taken place over the past few hours. So much had happened and now his life had changed dramatically. He could never have guessed when he awoke this morning, that in a short while he would be riding out beyond Graven with these two men. He thought about them and tried to imagine the life they had led up to this point. They were both much older than he was and he could tell by their faces that they were wise to the ways of the world, Drake probably more so than Flynn. Dorian was itching to ask Drake about the scar on his face, how he got it and why. He made up his mind to ask him at the first opportunity.

They rode at a steady pace for a few hours. Dorian found himself becoming accustomed to Fire, although occasionally the big stallion would want to break into a full gallop and had to be reined in. He obviously wanted to be in front and tossed his head every time Dorian held him back.

The path before them gradually became steeper and by mid afternoon, the horses had slowed to a trot. Dorian had the most peculiar sensation that someone or something was following them and tried to peer into the forest. He could not see more than a few feet in any direction, as the trees stood very closely together and the brush beneath was very dense. Should he say anything to the others?

Eventually the path became so steep and strewn with boulders that they found themselves walking. Drake brought his horse to a halt and dismounted. The other two did the same. The horses were exhausted and Dorian felt sore, hardly able to stand up straight.

'I think we should stop and let the horses rest for a while,' said Drake, 'there is a clearing a little further up with a pond.'

'Good idea,' said Flynn, 'we can break out the rations and have something to eat.'

They led their horses between the boulders and reached a level clearing carved out of the lee of the mountain. It was a small, circular area set into the rock. A little spring hung frozen above a man-made pond. Drake broke the thick layer of surface ice with the hilt of his sword.

The men drank first and filled their flasks, allowing the horses to drink after them. The water was cold but deliciously fresh. They slung bags of millet around the tired animal's necks allowing them to feed. The men ate nutty bread and strong cheese and sat down to rest a while.

'This water almost tastes sweet,' said Dorian. He had never been this far up before and was not used to water this pure.

'There's nothing like a mouthful of fresh, mountain spring water,' said Drake, 'once you have tasted it, nothing else compares.'

'Apart from a flagon of good Arillion red wine,' said Flynn with a smile.

The two men laughed and Dorian could not understand what was so funny. He looked from one to the other with a blank expression on his face. They stopped and cleared their throats.

'Yes, well maybe we will have to treat our friend here to the delights of the Arillion grape soon,' said Drake with a sparkle in his eye.

'I've had foreign wine before,' said Dorian, defensively, 'my uncle gets it from traders who come to Graven.'

Flynn was just about to say something when from out of the forest somewhere below them sprang a horrific sound. It sounded like some animal crying out in terrible pain.

'What was that?' asked Dorian.

'I don't know,' said Drake, his hand going to his dagger at his side, 'it sounded like a wolf. I thought I caught a glimpse of one in the woods a while back.'

'I've had this feeling . . . like we were being followed,' said Dorian.

The brothers exchanged an anxious glance.

'It's very important that you tell us of these feelings,' said Flynn sternly.

'I'll go and take a look,' said Drake. He turned to Flynn; 'you stay here with Dorian and guard the horses.'

Flynn nodded and without another word, Drake disappeared between the trees.

Dorian and Flynn sat in silence, the horses stamping and snorting every now and then. The minutes slowly ticked by and Dorian started to feel a little nervous. What was taking him so long?

They heard movement through the trees. They jumped to their feet and saw Drake appear, dashing towards them. An awful howling echoed up through the woods.

'We must make for the Houndsteeth at once!' Drake shouted with sweat pouring down his face. He had a wild look in his eyes that made Dorian feel a rush of fear.

'What is it?' asked Dorian with a start.

'I'll tell you as soon as we're away from here,' said Drake. He had obviously seen something he did not like and wasted no time mounting his horse. 'We must get higher up and out of the woods. I think we can ride from here, the path is clear of rocks as far as I can remember.'

The other two jumped into their saddles and followed Drake as he made his way up the path.

They forced the horses into a gallop and before long; a froth of sweat covered them, with steam swirling from their coats. The forest began to thin out and the terrain became more barren. They pressed on through until late afternoon.

The path changed from frozen, slippery mud to broken shale and levelled out into a broad highland that rose up before them. It was hard for Dorian to see much of the path as it began to blend into the expanse ahead. Here and there, lay pockets of snow with the odd solitary fir tree watching them in silence. Heavy, dark clouds hung overhead and the path rose to meet them about a league ahead. A thick mist began to roll down towards them. They slowed to a walk and fell in step beside each other.

'The entrance to the Houndsteeth lies up ahead,' panted Drake, looking over his shoulder at the way that they had come, 'we've made good time. Sunset is at least an hour away.'

'What was back there?' asked Flynn.

'Wolves,' said Drake, 'but there was something wrong with them.'

'What do you mean?' asked Dorian with a worried look on his face.

'They seemed crazed, almost demented. They were further down and had attacked one of their own. They caught scent of me and started up the mountainside. I didn't wait to see what they were about; it was obvious they were after my blood.'

'Strange behaviour for mountain wolves,' said Flynn.

'Yes indeed,' said Drake.

Dorian got the impression that Drake was not letting on about something. Just then, he had a vision of the wolves coming up behind them. In his mind, he could see their eyes, black and wild, their fangs dripping and exposed in a hideous grimace. The fangs looked bizarre. They were unnaturally grotesque. He could sense the wolves. They were in agony, exhausted and starving, but they were not hunting, they were forced . . . manipulated . . . and then he sensed something else . . . something evil!

A pitiful howl broke out behind them.

'They're upon us,' yelled Flynn, his hand going for his crossbow.

'Make for the gap,' shouted Drake as he spurred his horse into a gallop.

The others followed him without a moment's delay. Dorian looked back and caught a glimpse of the shadowy pack as it loped up the grade behind them, just as the thick fog engulfed their horses, swirling around them, murky and grey.

Their mounts were very exhausted but they laboured on. Two great fingers of rock loomed ahead of them. 'The Houndsteeth,' shouted Drake as he headed between them. They steered their way through, the wild howling too close for comfort.

'They're right behind us,' screamed Flynn, his horse whinnying in fear.

Dorian could not see much around him but he knew they had entered the pass. He could barely make out Drake's silhouette in front of him and tried to stay as close behind him as possible. They were on a narrow ledge as he could feel an icy wind blowing up from a great depth. The sound of the clattering hooves echoed all around them. He was terrified of possibly falling off the ledge or being trapped by the monstrous beasts should the path ahead be blocked. The only way was forward and Dorian willed Fire to keep his footing on the frozen rock beneath them. What were they to do? The ravenous wolves would surely attack them at any moment. He looked over his shoulder and shuddered at what he witnessed.

Through the fog, he saw Flynn's horse buck in horror as a dark shape pounced from behind. The poor animal made a terrible sound as one of the wolves sank its fangs into her back. Flynn was thrown against the rock-face and rolled forward. He found his feet and began to run towards them, a glint of steel in his right hand, crossbow in his left. 'Keep moving,' he yelled as he noticed Dorian hesitate.

Dorian's mind raced as he tried to decide what the best course of action should be. At that moment, he became aware of the Tamulus. It felt warm and it tingled against his flesh as if it had at once sprung to life at his beckoning. That familiar feeling of nausea wracked his stomach and he became dizzy. In an instant, he had a picture in his mind's eye of the immense rock face above them. His head swam as he battled to come to terms with its sheer size. He could see himself and his compatriots in flight with the pack attacking the grey mare behind. Flynn was a few paces ahead of the carnage, running for dear life. One of the creatures broke free of the pack and was now hot on Flynn's heels. It was almost as if Dorian were an eagle looking down at the scene below as he flew overhead. He was aware of everything around him, the cold rock, the wind, and the ice and snow . . . the snow above them in large pockets. He saw a drift of snow far above and ahead of them trapped between the rocks. There were loose boulders up there holding it back. He was not sure, if he was just imagining this out of sheer desperation or if the Tamulus was showing it to him. In any event, he was sure that if one of those small rocks up there somehow were to dislodge, it would cause an avalanche that might engulf the dangerous creatures behind them.

No sooner had he thought this than from above a dull rumble echoed. He heard Drake shouting something, but he was some way ahead and he could not make out the words as the rumbling grew louder and louder. He noticed Drake pointing up and beckoning wildly for them to hurry. He looked up, shocked by what he saw.

An avalanche had begun its perilous drive towards them. In seconds, the oncoming mass could sweep them from the ledge to an icy grave. Dorian dug his heels into Fire's flanks and flicked the reins in an attempt to spur the great steed on in one last burst of speed. There was an overhang up ahead that Drake had almost reached. Dorian knew it was their only hope of survival.

Rocks and snow pelted down around them and Fire charged ahead, tossing his mane wildly. The big stallion knew what was happening and managed to carry his rider to safety just as the bulk of mountain debris came down behind them with a tremendous crash. The sound trailed off down the ravine as the last small stones bounced off the ledge around them.

'By all the Gods of Creation,' exclaimed Drake, 'that was close. I was certain we were done-for one way or the other.'

'I know,' said Dorian, 'it looks like we're saved.' He looked around and felt a cold hand grip his heart. 'Where's Flynn?'

There was an eerie silence. They looked at each other and in the dim light Dorian could see the other man's face paled. 'I thought he was right behind you?' he said, peering over Dorian's shoulder in the hopes that Flynn might be there.

'I thought so too,' said Dorian as they dismounted carefully in the confined space and made their way back along the rock face.

Flynn and his horse had disappeared. They stood in silence and stared at the way they had come, now blocked by a wall of snow. Dorian felt a pang of guilt eat at his stomach. It was his fault. What if he had caused the avalanche, with the help of the Tamulus? He was almost certain he had. In a fit of rage, he grabbed at it wanting to rip it from his breast and throw it into the depths of the ravine below. As he clasped the Tamulus in his hand, he stood frozen, realising he could do no such thing. It had some kind of power over him. It was a part of him. He could be no freer of it than be bereft of an arm or a leg. They were destined for each other no matter what the consequence and he let go of it with a cry of grief.

Drake looked at him oddly and then turned and walked back a couple of paces to where the horses were, his head hung low in despair. 'It seems he is lost,' he said finally.

Dorian followed, not knowing whether he should try to say a kind word to comfort Drake or not. He had not known Flynn and decided it was best to keep quiet. Drake went to his stallion and put his hand on its neck as he worked at the saddlebag with the other. 'Good boy Brag,' he said as he stroked the horse's neck, 'those wolves nearly had us didn't they,' he turned to Dorian, 'I think we should spend the night here. The horses need to rest. This overhang should offer us protection from the weather and it is not as if anything can come upon us from behind. We shall hear anything approaching from yonder . . . at any rate, I will be alert.'

'You should try to get some sleep too Drake. I'll share the watch with you.'

'It won't be necessary. I sleep with one eye open.'

Dorian went to his saddlebag. There were two thin blankets. He threw one over Fire's back and gave him some sustenance. The black stallion snorted appreciatively and stamped his hind legs. 'They must be exhausted. We've driven them the entire day.'

'Yes we have,' said Drake, 'they're bred for it though.' He sounded sombre.

Dorian was not sure if he should say anything about his experiences with the Tamulus, the vision of the wolves and the avalanche, but finally decided to say nothing at all. Drake was obviously mourning his brother. Dorian shuddered at the notion of the awful fate that must have befallen Flynn and the fact that he himself may have had a hand in it.

They ate some salted meat and drank from a small flagon of wine that Drake produced. Dorian accepted it eagerly and relished the warmth that he felt seep through his freezing body. He was surprised at how good it was in comparison to the wine he had tasted at his uncle's inn in Graven. They sat huddled together, between the horses and the mountain, with their cloaks tightly wrapped about them.

Nightfall came swiftly to the mountains of Rega and in the pitch-blackness; they could barely hear the horses breathing close by as the freezing wind howled through the ravine.

'He was a good man and a brave soldier,' said Drake. It was the first thing he had said in a long while.

'Have you always served together?' ventured Dorian, carefully.

'We grew up together; he was my brother and we did everything together. We joined the military in Arillon together as youths. He saved my life once.'

'Oh?'

'It was nothing heroic,' said Drake, 'I was drunk and got into a brawl with a sailor in some tavern down in Karn . . . over some lass. We were much younger then.'

Dorian could hear a twinge of remorse in his voice. 'Is that how you got that scar?' he asked.

'Yes,' said Drake, 'I was so drunk that I could hardly stand up. This fellow had sliced my cheek clean through with his blade and would have cut my throat if Flynn hadn't cracked him over the head with a bottle.' He chuckled at the memory and Dorian smiled to himself at the thought. 'We shall meet again in the hereafter I suppose,' said Drake, distantly. 'Enough reminiscing let us get some rest.'

Dorian wanted to hear more of their past adventures but knew now was not the right time. He tried to get comfortable which proved an impossible task as the ground beneath them was hard and his body ached all over. The cold gnawed through to the bone. A thousand frightening images raced through his mind as he finally fell into a fitful sleep, dreaming of a brother he never had and then of Flynn lying crumpled and twisted beneath rock and snow in the ravine below.

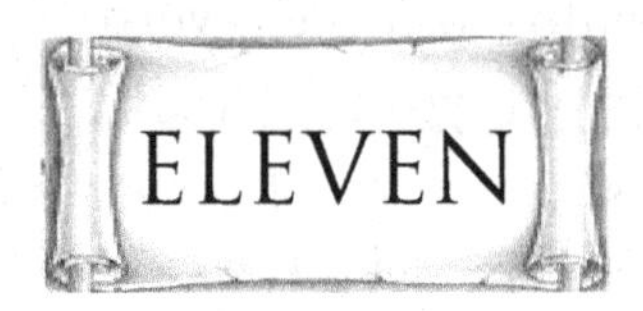

THE MOUNTAINS OF REGA

Dorian stirred as a hand shook him roughly by the shoulder. It was Drake. 'Time to leave,' he said as Dorian attempted to lift his stiff body off the ground. He looked about, uncertain of where he was for a moment. The memory of the previous evening's ordeal came flooding back to him. 'We must be on our way as soon as possible,' continued Drake, 'we have a long way to go before we can rest again.'

'I'm thirsty,' said Dorian, his voice thick with sleep.

'Drink some of this.' Drake handed him one of the calfskins of water. 'Don't drink too much . . . I'm not sure we'll find any running water up here for a while yet.'

Dorian took a few mouthfuls and finally managed to stand up. The air was thin and cold and he had difficulty breathing. It was just before dawn and he looked up at the heavens, surprised to see a few burning stars. 'The weather seems to have cleared. It looks like we may have a good day.'

'Don't be deceived,' said Drake, 'these mountains are renowned for extreme changes in weather, especially in winter, one minute it might be clear and the next a blizzard may descend upon you without warning.'

'I've heard a little about that from travellers who have come this way, although none of them have made it in winter. They always spoke of the summer rains and such.'

'This pass is usually far too dangerous to negotiate this time of year. Look at what happened last night. That stretch behind us is pretty much out of bounds until the spring thaw,' said Drake, nodding over his shoulder.

Dorian folded the blankets and then packed them away. He rummaged around trying to find something to eat. He gave Fire one of the sugar lumps he discovered in his pouch. 'You thought I'd forgotten about these, didn't you boy?' he said as the horse devoured the lump noisily. He gave one to Brag too, patting him on the neck.

'Never had one of those before,' said Drake.

'Oh, I'm sorry,' said Dorian stepping back from the stallion.

'It's all right; I just don't want him to get too used to them. We should eat something ourselves and get started.'

'I am desperate for a hot meal,' said Dorian, remembering the veritable feast they had enjoyed the previous morning at Graven Keep.

'I wouldn't count on one this morning,' remarked Drake, flatly.

They ate a few oatmeal cakes and then mounted their horses. The two men carefully made their way along the pass. Drake rode without saying another word. Dorian could sense his grief and left him with his thoughts in sympathy.

Dawn broke all around them in a purple wave reflecting off the glittering rock. Purple turned to orange and tongues of morning sunshine licked their way through the snow-capped peaks, the beauty of it astonishing Dorian.

Nothing but rock and blinding white ice surrounded them. A barren and desolate, yet majestic vista met the eye in all directions. The ledge on which they travelled wound its way ahead of them. It was probably just wide enough for a cart or small carriage. To their right the mountain rose at an incredible angle, its immediate upper reaches completely out of sight. To their left was a sheer drop into an immense ravine. Dorian dared not go too close to the edge to look down. Great dark and hostile looking mountains rose beyond this and it hurt his neck trying to catch a glimpse of the peaks above them. They had been going for about an hour when he thought he might venture a conversation. 'How deep is this valley?' he asked.

'It's called the Serpent's Rift,' said Drake, 'and it cuts a ravine a good few thousand feet deep between the mountains.'

Dorian gulped and guided Fire a little closer to the cliff face. 'Why is it called that?' asked Dorian.

'The Serpent's River flows down there, winding its way to the ocean. I suppose they named it after the way it snakes its way through the mountains.'

'And Rega is on the other side,' said Dorian, after a few minutes of silence.

'Yes, we are still in Voltar. The river forms a natural border between both kingdoms. You're an informed young man when it comes to geography aren't you?'

'My uncle had us tutored,' answered Dorian, sullenly.

'Well I didn't mean to insult you. You are obviously eager to learn . . . I'll be glad to answer any questions you might have. I've travelled much of Alton Savia.'

Dorian felt a little better about the way the conversation was going. He thought about the Serpent's River as it let out into the ocean at the furthermost tip of Voltar.

'I've learnt of the Borrowed River too,' he ventured brightly.

'Yes,' countered Drake, 'it's a tributary of this one and branches towards the coast within Voltar.

'Yes, south of Graven,' added Dorian. 'Have you ever been to *Mur*?' he asked, his thoughts turning to the Empress.

'No. Venturing across the Murian Straight has not been high on my agenda.'

'I wonder what it is like?' said Dorian, his mind conjuring up desert cities crouching under a haze of aromatic spices where men reared dragons and drank fiery liquor.

'There are old legends about men travelling by caravan to Muria in time for the sacrificial feasts that were so infamously held in the Empress's Lair. Most travellers were enslaved and only a handful made it back to tell the tale. In recent years Mur has apparently become more civilised and there is a vibrant sea trade with Arillon,' answered Drake, bleakly.

'How old is she?' asked Dorian.

'Who do you mean?' Drake asked, absently looking back over his shoulder.

'The Empress,' answered Dorian.

'Nobody knows exactly. It seems her evil powers have endured for over a hundred years, and she gains strength.'

Dorian thought about this for a while. He imagined an ugly old hag like some spider in her lair, preying on foreigners as if they were doomed flies caught in a web. 'Why is it called a *Lair*?' asked Dorian finally.

'I don't know,' said Drake simply, 'I think people call it that out of fear, it's apparently a fortress of sand and stone.'

They continued up the side of the mountain, the path before them becoming ever steeper and the air thinner. The sun started its climb towards its winter zenith and by mid morning, Dorian could feel its heat on his back. He began to sweat. They toiled ahead for another three hours.

'Up yonder lies the Great Arch,' said Drake after another long silence.

'Uh-huh,' said Dorian, not wanting to sound over excited.

Drake smiled to himself as he told Dorian that it was the crossing point into Rega.

Dorian was about to say he knew that, when they rounded another sweeping bend and his jaw dropped in awe at what lay before them.

It was truly a *great arch*. A massive stone structure curved across the ravine, joining two outcrops of rock that jutted from either side. This was the obvious point to build the arch, as beyond this the opposing sides of the mountains fell away again revealing more of the vast rift valley below. White stone gleamed in the wintry sunlight, hurting his eyes.

'We cross into Rega here,' said Drake, 'the going will be easier from this point as most of the climb is behind us.'

"Good news," thought Dorian to himself, and then aloud he asked, 'how much longer before we reach Ravencroft?'

'Another two days if the weather holds,' answered Drake as he stood at the entrance to the great bridge.

Off to one side stood a squat obelisk the colour of charcoal and on the side facing all who approached was an inscription carved in a language Dorian had never seen before.

'What does it say?' he asked.

'It is written in Regan,' Drake answered, 'and it reads . . .

"*Break not the bough*
Nor taint the stream
For surely shall thy
Fate be sealed"'

'It sounds like some kind of warning,' remarked Dorian.

'It is. They are very protective of their forest,' said Drake, leading the way across the bridge.

"It is an incredible view from up here," thought Dorian as he looked back down the ravine at the way they had come. The immense rift valley fell away into the distance and he could just see a twinkling line of water that snaked below them as the noon sun caught its surface.

'Pretty impressive isn't it,' said Drake.

'Yes,' answered Dorian, unable to say much more.

They both stood at the apex of the Great Arch mesmerised by the beauty of their surroundings. Dorian had the strangest feeling that someone was watching them and looked over to the other side, noticing a squat watchtower nestled between the rocks. He thought he saw movement through a tiny window high up.

'I think someone is up there in that tower watching us,' he said.

Drake immediately steered Brag towards the far side and drew his crossbow as he did so. 'Stay close to me,' he said.

Dorian followed Drake across to the other side and together they made their way between the rocks. Drake stopped and dismounted, silently indicating for Dorian to do the same. Dorian followed Drake as he led them off the track and between the huge rocky spears that eclipsed the tower before them. There were a few gnarled shrubs growing here, the first green plant life they had seen since the Houndsteeth. They fastened their reins to one of these and then crept towards the pathway that began a few paces ahead, leading up to the tower.

'No need for stealth,' boomed a voice from above, breaking into hearty laughter. 'Why it is I . . . Wurt!'

'You fool,' shouted Drake, 'why didn't you announce yourself earlier?'

The oddest sight confronted them as they came out into the open. Standing in the doorway of the watchtower above them was a very short, stout man with a great, red beard that reached almost to his waist. He wore a bright green jerkin with a matching pointed cap and on his back; he carried a large quiver of arrows. In his hand, he held a large bow and on his belt hung a scabbard with a dagger, the likes of which Dorian had never seen.

'Climb up here,' he said with a broad smile, 'you looks to me like cowering children down there.'

'I'll give you *cowering*,' said Drake as they climbed towards the tower.

'You and who's army,' was the retort. He had a strange accent and a slight lisp.

'Is he a dwarf?' asked Dorian, curiously, keeping his voice low.

'They don't like to be called dwarves,' answered Drake. 'He is Regan and his real name is Wurtel, but don't tell him I told you so,' he said with a measure of mischief.

They reached the top to have their hands shaken vigorously by the small man.

'You must be master Dorian,' said Wurt as he ushered them into the damp gloom of the tower.

'Yes,' answered Dorian, 'I believe I still am.'

'Well 'tis a great pleasure to meet you Sire,' he said.

'Sire?' asked Dorian perplexed.

'Uh . . . what brings you to these parts?' interjected Drake.

'Morgan dispatched me to meet you,' said Wurt, his face becoming serious, 'let us sit aloft for a while . . . we must speak.'

They followed Wurt up the winding staircase and reached a room in the uppermost part of the tower, where they sat on old ramshackle benches. No sooner had they sat down than the little man jumped up to go over to the window and peer out, as if someone may have been following them. He sniffed at the air.

'What is wrong my friend?' asked Drake.

Wurt looked from one to the other and then came over to whisper almost in their faces, 'There is a *Blackwraith* afoot.'

'A *what?*' asked Dorian, uneasily.

'I thought as much,' said Drake, 'it looks like this isn't going to be as easy as I had hoped.'

'What is a *Blackwraith?*' asked Dorian, becoming agitated.

'It's hard to explain this to you now,' answered Drake.

'I seem to be hearing a lot of that.'

'It is an assassin hailing from Mur,' said Drake.

'Yes, an evil monstrosity that only that lunatic queen of the Godforsaken northlands could conjure up,' said Wurt as he spat on the floor in disgust.

'It is believed there is a sect of her followers who have the ability to leave their human bodies and enter or possess other living things. In this way they use their dark power to manipulate their host to their own, or rather *her* evil ends,' explained Drake.

'The wolves!' said Dorian.

'Exactly!' remarked Drake, 'the poor creatures. They didn't stand a chance.'

'But there was more than one wolf,' noted Dorian.

'The Blackwraith has the ability to command more than one victim of a lower species,' said Drake. 'Man proves to be more of a challenge. A powerful wraith may possess a man depending on the strength of his will to fight back.'

'Disgusting things,' said Wurt, acidly.

'I've never known one to get this far south,' said Drake.

'Morgan got wind of it by raven from Voltar Regis. He sent me to warn you and to escort you back to him in safety,' said Wurt, pushing his chest out.

'My friend here is a formidable mercenary,' said Drake with a smile. 'He's had a run in with one before.'

'And I hope it never happens again,' said Wurt with a shudder. 'What of Flynn,' he continued, 'I thought he would be with you?'

Dorian looked at Drake and noticed sadness in his eyes again.

'He was lost in an avalanche while we were under attack in the pass,' said Drake, solemnly. He told Wurt of their ordeal.

'By the Gods, I am truly sorry for your loss,' said Wurt, 'he was a good man.' He placed one hand on his chest and the other on Drake's shoulder in a sign of respect and condolence.

'One of the best,' said Drake.

There was a moment of silence as Drake looked away from them to hide his grief. Wurt stood back sensing his pain.

'Morgan believes the wraith has been sent to prevent *him* from reaching Arillon,' said Wurt, nodding at Dorian.

'Well it's going to have a tough time now that we are aware of it,' said Drake, 'we have an advantage.'

'How so?' asked Dorian.

'You see, it has to leave its own body within a certain radius of its flight. We could sniff it out and destroy it,' said Wurt, triumphantly raising his fists above his head.

'It's not as simple as that,' said Drake, 'but that is the general idea. Destroying the body is not the end of it.'

'How so?' asked Dorian.

'The body is just a vessel. The evil soul will just be released to wander.'

'How do we *sniff* it out?' asked Dorian.

'Exactly so,' said Wurt, 'with my nose.' He stuck his nose in the air and sniffed. 'Hmm . . . it's way off, but it's here.'

'You can *smell* it?' Dorian was surprised.

'You will too when you get up close,' said Wurt.

'Wurt here comes from a long line of true Regan mountain men. They are renowned for their sense of smell,' said Drake patting the short man's shoulder.

'Not to mention their accuracy with a bow and arrow and their love of wine, women and song,' said Wurt, gleefully.

'Just so,' said Drake, and then on a serious note, 'The Blackwraith will usually hide itself in a safe place before leaving its body.'

'Not that safe,' added Wurt, with a wry smile.

'They start out as men, but once they become devout followers of the Obsidian Order, or *Gordus Murdim*, they achieve the status of Blackwraith. The dark forces overwhelm them and they become so obsessed with leaving their own bodies that they do exactly that as much as they possibly can. The dark power twists and torments their true form and they begin to prematurely wither and age. It is the Mask that keeps them alive and invariably they become wracked with disease and neglect—hence the smell,' said Drake.

'Not a pretty sight,' said Wurt with a shudder.

'Where does the soul go once the body has been destroyed?' asked Dorian wide-eyed.

'I believe the soul roves the earth, inhabiting creatures that can be commandeered, constantly under the influence of the Mask. With the loss of its own body it will look for another host,' explained Drake. 'Maybe even a human one.'

'They are driven by the will of the Mask for eternity,' said Wurt dryly.

Drake gazed up at a ray of wintry sunlight that filtered through the tiny window above them, and then down at the cold stone floor as it grappled between the cracks. 'The power of evil can be deceiving and all consuming,' he said solemnly. Everyone sat in silence for a few moments pondering Drake's words.

'I'm hungry,' said Dorian. The talk of rotting bodies had made his stomach churn and rumble and he thought some bread and cheese might make him feel better. He had broken the spell and now everyone stood up.

'Yes, some lunch is a good idea,' said Drake, 'we'll feed the horses too and then head north as soon as possible. The Sacred Wood lies ahead of us and will afford us some protection from the cold night air up here.'

'Are we not to seek out that blasted Wraith?' asked Wurt with a tinge of disappointment.

'I think not,' said Drake. 'It would be better to make for Ravencroft as soon as possible. Any delay may put us in more danger than is necessary.'

'I'll feed the horses,' said Dorian, 'and collect our saddle bags.' He left the small room and headed down the moss-covered stairwell, leaving the other two to talk. Their muted tones echoed behind him as he left the watchtower and made his way down the path.

Dorian found the horses nibbling on the shrubs they were tethered to. 'You must be hungry my friends,' he said as he hung the feedbags around their necks. As he began unfastening the saddlebags, he felt a warm sensation against his chest.

It was the Tamulus.

He had almost forgotten that it was there, but now that he was out in the open and by himself, he became aware of it. It was almost as if it was letting him know that he was not alone out here. He felt secure in the knowledge that it was with him, protecting him from any danger that might lurk among the rocks . . . and then he got the impression that he was in some kind of danger, and that he should get back to the others as soon as possible.

He grabbed the saddlebags and quickly made his way back up to the tower. Both Drake and Wurt looked at him expectantly as he burst into the room panting.

'What is it?' asked Drake, jumping to his feet.

'I don't know,' answered Dorian, 'I suddenly felt like there was something out there.'

Wurt went over to the window and peered out again, taking in a chest full of mountain air. 'The coast seems to be clear; I don't smell anything out there but the horses and a lot of damp rock.'

'Hmm, I think we should eat and leave right away,' said Drake, 'and I think in future you should stay as close to us as possible. It was a bit stupid of me to let you go down there on your own in the first place.'

DANGER IN THE NIGHT

After a meagre lunch, they went down to their horses. Wurt brought his mount from behind the tower. Dorian thought it quite comical as the little man appeared astride what was a midget of a horse. A miniature version of a normal horse in every sense, apart from the head, that looked a bit like a donkey's.

'Her name is Daisy,' said Wurt as he gallantly trotted down the path, glaring at Dorian's obvious amusement, 'and don't you be giving her that look young man, she is sensitive.'

Dorian quickly wiped the smile off his face with an evasive gesture of his left hand, 'I'm sorry,' he said, 'it's just that I've never seen one like her before.'

'She is a thoroughbred Regan pony,' said Drake, 'incredibly fast and sturdy for their size.'

'Not to mention incredibly intelligent and moody,' added Wurt as he joined them at the foot of the path.

Dorian was almost sure that Daisy had given him a cold sidelong glance as she stopped in the shadow of Fire.

'Let us be away then, shall we,' said Wurt, leading them between the black rocks and away from the tower.

The newly formed trio filed along the path and soon began to descend towards an enormous forest. It stretched below them into the distance like a thick, green carpet rolled out between the mountains that ranged to either side. Soon they were trotting between the trees and Dorian noticed the eerie silence about them. 'What a strange place,' he said, 'it's awfully quiet. Where are all the birds?'

'Birds?' repeated Wurt, 'oh they're about. They're just keeping still as we pass. Not much traffic through here you know. We are strangers in their peaceful world.'

'I see,' said Dorian, although he thought it odd. The birds back in Graven made a racket all the time.

'Rega is a quiet and mysterious place,' said Drake, 'you don't often see or hear much at all. Even the Regan people don't like to show themselves unless it is absolutely necessary.'

'Where are their villages?' enquired Dorian.

'Ah, you shan't find them too quickly,' answered Wurt, proudly, 'we adore the inviolability of our mother forest and prefer to remain concealed from outside eyes.'

Dorian reflected on this for a while and then asked, 'Do you not like other races?'

'Oh I wouldn't be saying that,' said Wurt, 'we are a nation that prefers our own company that is all. Solitude and oneness with nature are our hallmarks.'

'But you fought with Voltar against the hordes of Traal?' countered Dorian.

'That was at the request of the King of Voltar,' interjected Drake, a little taken aback by the young man's directness.

'It was to protect our sovereignty too,' said Wurt, 'we could not allow that mad bunch of evil hooligans to come stomping through here.'

Dorian smiled at the little man's fierce demeanour as he described the enemy that might have invaded his homeland. He was obviously fond of his forest and his Regan passion for sovereignty impressed Dorian.

They chatted amongst themselves as the day wore on and it soon became evident to Dorian that he could not tell what time of day it was. The dense green canopy above blocked out most of the light. He thought it must be near sunset as the light waned completely and before long they were plunged into darkness.

'We should set up camp for the night,' said Drake, echoing Dorian's thoughts as they came to a standstill.

'I know of a clearing up ahead,' offered Wurt, 'follow me.'

He led them off the path and into the woods. Dorian was amazed at how he knew his way about, as the forest was now almost as black as pitch and even the nearest trees were nothing but shadows cast upon even darker ones.

They soon entered a clearing and the horses came to a halt in unison, he heard the sounds of the others dismounting.

'I will light a fire,' said Wurt out of nowhere as Dorian slid from his horse's saddle. He heard a scraping sound as Wurt cleared a space on the ground and then, in an instant, the forest around them sprang to life. Wurt had struck the tinderbox and flames had caught the small pile of raked kindling. 'We shall have to gather more wood,' Wurt said.

They went about collecting dry twigs and branches and stacked them in a pile a few paces from where they set up camp.

After feeding the horses they settled down around the warmth of Wurt's handiwork as the cold night air seeped through the trunks around them. Dorian shivered and pulled his cloak tightly around his knees, staring into the burning pile of tinder. 'Are we safe here?' he asked, mesmerised by the flames that danced before him.

'There is nothing nor nobody for leagues in all directions,' said Wurt, 'we are in the heart of The Sacred Wood, and she will shield us from the night.' He sniffed at the air.

'You love this place don't you?' remarked Dorian as he looked up and witnessed their tall shadows bob from great bole to bole in the background.

'She is our guardian and friend and our knowledge of her is a secret we treasure. We worship her; she is the Goddess of Rega. Her spirits live in the trees and manifest only to the most worthy.' He said this with a reverence that hung in the air like a prayer.

'We too worship her indirectly I suppose,' said Dorian, in acknowledgment, 'as we follow the Earth-Goddess Mia.'

'We should be getting some sleep,' said Drake, 'I do not mean to spoil the conversation, but we have another long ride ahead of us tomorrow.'

'Too right,' said Wurt, 'I shall take the first watch.'

The three men made themselves comfortable and Dorian drifted off to sleep in the warmth of the fire, watching the shadows as they flickered and bounced around him like a ring of pretty maidens clasping hands in a spiral ritual.

In the dead of night, Dorian dreamed of many things. A story unfolded in his mind; in it, he became aware of a prowling entity that sniffed them out. A chillingly sad cry of pain rent the woods.

He jolted upright and wide-awake to see a figure standing over him. The flames had dwindled to a few glowing embers.

'What the . . .' he said with a start.

'Shhhh!' it was Drake with his finger to his lips. He crouched beside Dorian and whispered in his ear, 'there is something nearby.'

'What is it?' asked Dorian, under his breath. He looked about and noticed that Wurt was missing. 'Where is Wurt?'

'He has gone to investigate.'

They sat in absolute silence and then heard the sound of feet trampling through the woods.

Drake drew his dagger and peered out into the night. The trees stood shoulder to shoulder around them like tall, dark, red sentries, as if to ward off any would-be intruder.

All at once, a figure stumbled into the clearing and they jumped to their feet in surprise. To their abject horror, Flynn fell to the ground at their feet. He was shaking, weak, and covered in a cold sweat.

'By all the Gods!' said Drake as he rushed to Flynn's side.

Flynn's eyes rolled back in his head and he looked emaciated and pale. Dorian threw his blanket around him and looked at Drake in shock. 'What is wrong with him?' he asked.

'He looks exhausted,' answered Drake.

'But how could he have followed us here on *foot*?'

'I have no idea,' said Drake, perplexed.

Just then, all hell broke loose as Wurt appeared in the circle of dim light from the tree line. He lunged towards Flynn with his axe in hand but the stony white form of the exhausted Flynn rose to his feet like a stiff corpse, as if a string drew him up, and shot towards Dorian, his dagger in his hand. A shrill gurgling scream erupted from deep inside him.

'Watch out,' screamed Wurt.

At the same time, the Tamulus sprang to life close to Dorian's heart and he became aware of a dark power that had entered Flynn's body. The Blackwraith was within the poor man and he could feel its malice towards him emanating from Flynn's mind like a savage beast with the sole intent of destroying him.

'WATCH OUT!' yelled Drake as he wrestled Flynn to the ground.

Dorian sprang back in fear and then almost as suddenly felt a rush of anger well up inside of him. It was so strong that he could not help but let it loose towards the creature. With a vengeance of willpower that tore through the air like a ton of bricks, producing a deafening kinetic crack that shook the ground, his force of reckoning struck at the heart of the beast. A bright flash of crimson light sprang across the clearing. It had originated from the heart of the Tamulus and it appeared like a bolt of lightning that connected with Flynn. In his mind, Dorian perceived a cold, black pit of evil filled with a writhing entity.

An agonising shriek rent through the Sacred Wood and surrounded them on all sides, as the loathsome thing recoiled in horror and fled from the impact of Dorian's rage. The sound was awful and beat a hasty retreat as it echoed through the trees.

Flynn's body went limp in Drake's arms and a long sigh escaped from his lips like a release of pain so deep that it sounded like he had left this earthly plane.

'Is he dead?' asked Dorian, shaking in his boots.

'His heart still beats,' answered Drake, his hand on his brother's chest, 'but ever so faintly. It must have driven him here and then lurked inside him waiting to pounce.'

'Will he be all right?'

'I don't know; we will have to take him to Morgan. He will know what to do.'

'I'm not sure of what just happened, but I hope I never have to experience that again,' said Dorian, trembling.

'I think you have started to learn the ways of the Wielding,' said Drake as he threw a couple of branches onto the burning heap and then dragged Flynn's prostrate form near to it. 'We need to keep him warm. He has survived this attack, but just barely. That vile thing has poisoned his mind and soul. He *will* live through this.' For the first time Dorian saw fear in Drake's eyes.

'You have wielded it away!' Wurt sounded impressed and had a very big grin on his face.

Dorian had to sit down, as he felt weak. He began to wretch uncontrollably as his stomach convulsed in shock. He was shaking as Wurt came over and passed Dorian his water. He accepted it gratefully, rinsing his mouth before slowly quenching his thirst.

'Are you all right?' asked Drake.

'I think so. I feel dreadful,' he quavered, 'almost as if I had eaten something bad.'

'It will pass,' offered Drake, 'I have seen this before.'

'You have . . . with whom?'

'Someone I served many years ago.' Drake turned and walked to the perimeter of the clearing, cocking his head to one side, seemingly listening out for something.

Dorian lay back exhausted. Unable to pursue the discussion, he fell asleep.

He awoke to the sounds of voices that filtered down to him through a fine dawn haze. The early morning light was pale and grey. Frost clung to his cloak as he lifted himself onto his elbows to see Drake and Wurt deep in conversation. Flynn was still lying unconscious where he had been left, next to the now completely burnt out campfire.

'We should make it by late afternoon,' Wurt was saying.

'I had better wake him,' said Drake, 'I think he should have rested long enough.'

'Pretty impressive stuff, what with him wielding that kind of power already,' continued Wurt.

'It took a lot out of him; he's going to have to get a lot better before we go into battle. Who knows what kind of force may be thrown at us once she realises he's still alive.'

'Battle?' asked Dorian as he stood up groggily, wiping the sleep out of his eyes.

'Ah, you're awake. Good. We have to leave right now,' said Drake. Dorian thought he seemed elusive. Perhaps he realised Dorian may have heard their conversation.

'What am I, some kind of secret weapon that you are required to get to the battlefield post-haste? Is that it gentlemen?'

'No need for sarcasm Dorian. All of your questions will be answered this evening I'm sure,' said Wurt as he moved to the horses.

It was then that Dorian noticed that blood covered Wurt from head to toe.

'What happened to you?' he asked.

'He had a run in with a boar,' laughed Drake.

'What?' asked Dorian.

'After you chased that creature out of Flynn's body it had to go somewhere. It escaped into a wild boar that was foraging a ways from here. I had to dispose of the poor beast too but I was trying to track the Blackwraith back to its source. I wanted to find the lecherous body and murder it for good. But I could not find it after it left the boar.'

'You killed a wild boar with your bare hands? But how did you know it had gone into the boar?' Dorian asked.

'It's difficult to explain. It is as if the trees showed me and I could sense it. I also heard the pig squeal with fright as the

Blackwraith commandeered it directly after leaving Flynn. I then tracked it. It was nothing,' said Wurt with a smile as he hoisted his saddlebags onto the pony. Daisy got a bit skittish as she sniffed at the blood all over him. 'It's all right my girl,' he soothed. 'I know; I need to bathe.' He turned to the others and said, 'I just wish we could have found that dreadful thing's body. It must have left its body way back somewhere before it commanded Flynn. I found no scent of it in the woods.'

'No matter now my man, it would be best if we left this place. With a bit of luck we'll all have a hot bath and a good meal tonight,' said Drake. Turning to Dorian, he continued, 'you and I will have to take turns carrying Flynn on our horses, I'll go first.'

The other two helped Drake lift Flynn onto Brag's back, wrapping him up warmly, and fastening him down like a large sack of potatoes. His complexion was the colour of ash and gleamed with an oily sweat as if taken by a terrible fever.

'He doesn't look at all well,' remarked Dorian, 'do you think we will reach Ravencroft in time?'

'He is strong and the fact that he has survived this ordeal thus far is testament to his willpower.' Drake was emphatic, 'he *will* make it.'

Dorian glanced at Wurt who smiled in return saying, 'that is the calibre one would expect of a soldier of Arillon.' He attempted to clean himself up as best he could with damp leaves, burying them in a shallow hole, along with the remnants of the previous night's campfire. 'We don't want to leave any sign of our passing,' he said, as he led them off through the dawn forest.

It was not long before they found the trail and continued their sojourn through the woods. The sun had risen now as Dorian could see the odd ray of light break through the canopy, to dabble a while and then disappear as if a thick green curtain had been drawn in front of them. The day wore on and at mid-morning, they transferred Flynn to Fire's back. Fire seemed a little put out by the whole affair. Flynn never stirred and Drake regularly touched his unconscious brother's back to see if he was still breathing.

The prospect of reaching Ravencroft thrilled Dorian. He was anxious to hear the truth about his origins. The secrecy surrounding his true father's identity confused him. Why could they not just tell him outright? Maybe he was a spy or even an outlaw; in any event, it would be interesting news. The whole experience perplexed Dorian and so many questions entered his mind. His thoughts rested on a lovely hot meal with wine or mead and a soft, warm bed. He was exhausted and could feel that the horses were as well. They trundled on, eating a little as they rode and talking at times about the previous night. Dorian tried to imagine what had become of the Blackwraith and whether it could have made it back to its own body. He shivered at the thought of it haunting its way through the woods. They all agreed that the sooner they reached Ravencroft, the better.

AN UNEXPECTED MESSAGE

Captain Goran Wilbur-Axe contemplated the message he had just penned on the small scroll of paper. The afternoon sun played cat and mouse with the dark clouds above and long shadows appeared intermittently across the ramparts. He hated being the bearer of this sad news; that one of the young men in the service of the king of Voltar had lost his life in the line of duty at the hands of a *Blackwraith*. He reflected on the future and the many other men of Voltar that now marched into war. More importantly, his message contained the news that the Lord Tarrant, grand prelate to the throne of Voltar, was in fact a traitor. He conspired with the unclean order *Gordus Murdim* that had vexed the continent with its evil fanaticism and unnatural practices.

How things had changed over the years. He still remembered a time when peace ruled throughout Alton Savia and a man knew where he stood. There was so much bad news coming out of Arillon these days and he, like so many, blamed Dragar's advent to the throne as the grounds for the widespread discontent. How had this state of affairs transpired? Why was there an alliance with Mur without the approval of the sister kingdoms? There were spies running around throughout the land and more worrying than that, the horror of the Blackwraiths was now unleashed upon an innocent populace.

He rolled the parchment into the capsule and attached it to the raven's leg. The bird squawked and flapped its wings in protest. Once he had secured the capsule, he lifted the bird from its cage and in a swift movement released the avian messenger into the heavens. 'Find your way home my friend,' he shouted as the blue-black form found its wings and headed northeast.

'A trusty soldier.' Gwyneth stood in the archway to the aviary in the northern tower.

'Yes, a true disciple in the service of Ravencroft,' he added with a half-smile.

'Will he reach his mark?' she asked with a touch of concern.

'He should do my Lady,' he answered, 'he has never failed me before.'

'The day draws to a close. When do you think we should leave?'

He had decided that it would be best to allow Gwyneth to accompany him and his men on the ride back to the king's army. Arguing had been futile, as the princess had made up her mind and under the circumstances, it was pointless expecting that she would stay within the confines of these walls. It was a prison to her, without a primary gatekeeper and warden. There was nobody to stop her from escaping and he thought it better to have her close. He had thought it through and he was certain his king would agree.

'The sooner the better, they will be making camp for nightfall. If we leave soon we can make it before they break camp tomorrow morning. We would do well to be careful and I have seconded four guards who will accompany us. We may encounter danger on this ride.'

'That is a wise decision,' she agreed.

'Do you have confidence in your mount?'

'Breeze can make it. What of your steed?'

'He will be fine and Bryn too. They have both watered and fed and the last few hours of rest will have stood them in good stead for our sojourn into the hinterland,' he answered.

'I shall give the word to have our rides made ready. I ordered the preparations earlier and our supplies ought to be ready soon,' Gwyneth offered.

'Thank you my Lady.' Goran looked away, seemingly distracted.

'I truly am sorry for the loss of Mark,' she said, laying a hand on the grieving man's shoulder.

He tried to hide the feelings that he knew were so evident. 'Thank you my Lady,' he smiled and then broke from her touch, 'we have much to do before we leave and I must check on my animals.'

'Yes of course,' she said as she let him pass. "He is such a good man," she thought, "a captain with the heart of a lion, but the sensibilities of a nobleman."

Six riders and a wolfhound stole through the alleyways of Voltar Regis; they decided to take the road less travelled. They disguised themselves as much as possible to look like a nondescript group of travellers. They wore plain, grey hooded cloaks and kept their faces covered as they left the city in the early winter dusk. Smoke from the many chimneys around them hung in the air above the empty streets and alleyways, most people were indoors for warmth and the usual evening family routine. They inhaled the many smells of food being prepared as they moved towards the city gates and Goran wished he could partake of something hearty and warm.

After passing through the gates without incident, they headed along the northern road towards the edges of the Sacred Wood. The army had headed this way instead of taking the usual way around the mountains to the east. King William had decided that the forest and Mountains of Rega would offer better cover on their approach to Caledon. There were also no settlements this way and with luck, they would avoid any prying eyes. It would be harder on the men and their animals negotiating the mountains and rough terrain but it was a price worth paying for the element of surprise.

Inside of two hours, they reached the forest and entered a dark world of merging shadows and unnerving silence. Two of the castle guard lit small oil lanterns and raised them aloft on reed staffs. The guards secured the staffs to the back of their saddles and the light provided, as the lamps bobbed above them, was sufficient to see a few yards ahead. This was a Regan contraption called a *doula*. The dwarves devised it for use when travelling through the Sacred Wood at night. They followed the trail between the trees and tried to maintain a steady pace.

A cold wind whistled through the trees and tore through their clothing, chilling Gwyneth to her core. The warmth of Breeze beneath her was the only comfort in an otherwise unforgiving environment and she actually found herself longing for her warm bed in her very comfortable tower chamber. After another hour, they came upon a stream that trickled along a rocky seam, interrupting the thick mantle of dense green.

'Let us break for a drink here,' said Goran, as he reined in his steed, bringing the party to a halt.

'What a cold and windy place we find ourselves in,' said Gwyneth, dryly.

'Indeed,' said Goran, 'I could think of a few better places to be on this dark, cold night.'

'Yes I was thinking that exactly,' she smiled.

Everyone dismounted; they let the horses drink from the stream and filled their calfskins with water. The men chatted amongst themselves and broke into their rations. Bryn lay panting between the horses and looked somewhat exhausted already.

'I may have to gather him up and let him ride with me for a while,' commented Goran.

'He rides with you?' she asked, incredulously.

'Yes, I have trained him since he was a pup. He doesn't always like it but he knows sometimes that it is the better option until he is rested, especially on long journeys such as this.'

Just then, they heard a deep growl coming from the wolfhound. He stood up now, intent on the tree line on the other side of the stream. His hair stood on end like a cat that had taken fright.

'What is it boy,' whispered his master, 'what vexes you so?'

'Must be a poisonous frog,' quipped one of the guards.

'Methinks your poisonous gasses,' added a second and they all laughed in merriment.

'No, I think there is something over there,' said Gwyneth, seriously. The laughing stopped and they all looked in the direction she indicated. At first, it seemed there was nothing there apart from the light from the doula, which cast a dim yellow hue.

'What in Mia's name is that?' One of the guards stepped back in dismay pointing at a glowing mist across the stream. As he did so, they all gasped at the inexplicable vision appearing right before their eyes. A haze rose up between the oak trees.

The vapour glowed with an uncanny green light as if there was a hidden arrangement of lamps within the trees. The miasma began to coalesce into a single pillar and then, astonishingly it became evident that there was a human form manifesting. It was the figure of a woman.

'Stand back,' Goran warned as he drew his sword and the men of the guard followed suit.

Gwyneth, however, felt a sense of tranquillity befall her and she ordered them to stand down. 'No it is all right,' she said, taking a step closer.

'What is it my Lady?' enquired Goran.

'I am not sure,' she answered, 'but I sense that it means us no harm.' She could not explain her intuition.

As they stared in disbelief at this apparition that had materialized out of the ether, they realised that the woman was naked. Her complexion was very pale and her figure slender. She had lustrous, verdant hair that cascaded to her waist covering her breasts as it fell. It was hard to tell whether it was hair or gleaming moss filled with a myriad of diminutive leaves that shed from her as she stood. She had a beautiful face by any standard with bright jade eyes that shone like stars in a velvet firmament. Her skin sparkled as if covered in a thousand tiny crystals. A wisp of a smile lingered at the corner of her perfectly formed mouth. It was as though a bright full moon had broken through to shine only upon her.

The men sighed, transfixed in a dreamlike state. Even Bryn went from being an aggressor to a supine pup. "What is this strange magic that holds these men in a trance so?" thought Gwyneth as she moved forward for a closer look.

'Who are you?' asked Gwyneth.

"I am Celestria," answered the vision before her. Gwyneth did not see her lips moving. She could hear the satin whisper of

a voice in her head. The voice spoke to her alone and did not resonate in the physical world between them.

'I can hear you, and yet you do not speak,' said Gwyneth aloud.

"I speak only to you my Lady," said Celestria.

'*What* are you?' asked Gwyneth.

"I am the spirit and keeper of the trees," was the reply.

'A Dryad?' asked Gwyneth, surprised.

"You may call me that," intoned the voice in her mind.

"Can you hear my thoughts as I can hear yours?"

"Yes my Lady."

"What has happened to my men?"

"They are enchanted and will be in a dream for a moment. They are not privy to this conversation and will have only vague recollections of this event afterwards," said Celestria.

'What do you want of me?' asked Gwyneth aloud.

"I mean you no harm and have come to you as the bearer of news that will aid you in your quest. In so doing I also serve the will of the Sacred Wood."

'What do you mean?'

"We have sensed an evil presence in the realm of trees and we are concerned for the sanctity of our dominion. You must take heed of my utterances and safeguard your future as well as ours."

'What would you have me do?' Gwyneth asked, earnestly.

"You are heading for Arillon are you not?"

'Yes that we are.'

"When you near your destination it is important that you do not leave the Wood. My sisters have informed me that there is danger, which lies beyond. I have witnessed a dark and destructive presence pass through here to the foothills of the Drakenstein in Arillon. It was careful to circumvent the army of Voltar and passed on into Caledon."

'Do you mean Tarrant or the Blackwraith?'

"Yes, we have felt the unclean. Do not leave the Wood. We can hide you from the evil gaze that searches for you as long as you remain within our trees. You must amass your armies within our bosom until the one true king returns as the prophecies have foreseen. You must warn your father before the sun rises on the morrow."

'I do not follow, who is the one true king?'

"The holder of the stone is near. We have felt his presence and that of the Bloodstone he bears. He makes for the house of the ravens and the free one. You need protection until his union with Disparager and the eye and the heart are one. This is your destiny." The form began to fade.

'Wait, what of the Regan army, they mean to join my father's forces?'

"They too are shielded, but must also stay within the wood." The Dryad dissolved into the darkened forest and her voice echoed through the trees as she left. Gwyneth thought of the whisper of tinkling bells receding on a clear spring day. When the apparition had completely disappeared, she stood contemplating the conversation she had just had. Her mind raced as she tried to fathom the gravity of the message. She had to warn her father as a matter of urgency. They would have to ride like demons to get to him before the dawn.

The men and the hound came to their senses and looked at each other with the recognition of a child awakening from a deep slumber to find a sibling nearby.

'What happened?' asked Goran.

'We have been forewarned. A visitation by a Dryad,' said Gwyneth ardently, 'we must make haste. She mentioned the prophecy and a danger to our armies. I must inform my father before the sun rises.'

'Yes, my mind is clouded but I remember vaguely. It seems my memory fails me as to the finer details,' said Goran.

'You were under her spell. You all were, even Bryn.'

'These are bizarre times my Lady. I have heard of the Dryads but never believed we would encounter one. They only appear in times of trouble to forewarn those burdened with a troublesome fate. We should take heed and make haste to convey the message.'

They raced through the night, pushing their horses as hard as they could. In the early hours of the morning, just before the sun threatened the eastern horizon, they passed through Hoth's Gate in the Drakenstein and came upon a sight that made their hearts sing. Below them among the trees of the Sacred Wood, they could see the burning campfires of the Voltarian army. Gwyneth was relieved that the armies had set up here, as they were still a few leagues from the edge of the wood. The lookouts confronted them before they reached the tented encampment, as the party approached quietly. After identifying themselves, a scout escorted them to the king's marquee. As they passed through the camp, Gwyneth looked up at the trailing blue and white banners of Voltar flying alongside the purple and black of Rega. A sense of hope filled her.

THE LESSON

Jeb and a handful of lads his age had spent many days in training with their new master and the master's hand, Shram. The prelate's subordinates fed, housed, and taught the boys how to handle weapons. He enjoyed this training and all the lessons on how to be a scout in the army. They were too young to go to war but he and his counterparts were good for running errands. The training he did not enjoy at all was with the Lord Tarrant. Every time he went into the prelate's chamber, he felt an uncomfortable sickness in the pit of his stomach. When his lessons ended and he left, the feeling would diminish and eventually disappear after a period. The worst part of it all was that he could never remember what the content of the lessons had been. This state of affairs always left him feeling empty and dubiously uneasy.

Today was to be another day of lessons with his master and a guard would be collecting him shortly. He sat on his low bunk in the long room that served as sleeping quarters to all Lord Tarrant's new conscripts. He had been thinking about the other children who had sailed with him from Karn and desperately needed to know what had become of them. He had not seen them since they arrived and felt badly about the situation. He remembered seeing the two boys in the cage down below in the dungeons and hoped that they were being looked after as well as he was. There was also the little Sara and the memory of her fearful face as he was separated from her, haunted him. Today he was going to ask after them. He thought he might ask Oonagh, as she would probably be the one with relevant information. She was responsible for feeding his troop and would surely be responsible for the other children too.

The guard arrived and escorted him through the maze of passages to the prelate's apartments. When he arrived, the tall, thin man was sitting at his reading desk studying a map. The guard announced Jeb's entrance and Lord Tarrant looked up. 'Ah,' he said, 'you are here, good, good.'

'Yes m' lord,' answered Jeb as the guard took his leave, closing the doors as he did so.

'Shram informs me that you have proven yourself to be a very competent young apprentice and that your instruction as a scout is advancing most excellently,' his bushy eyebrows seemingly at odds with one another as one crept skywards.

'Yes m' lord,' Jeb mumbled.

'Don't mumble boy!'

'Sorry m' lord,' his tone elevated this time, to appease.

'Tell me what you know of the war,' Tarrant demanded.

'Only what I have heard in Karn m' lord,' answered Jeb, not quite sure what he was supposed to have knowledge of.

'Well what have you heard?' Lord Tarrant sounded peeved.

'Um, that there is discontent within Alton Savia and the alliance is in danger of being broken,' he offered tentatively.

'And where does this danger stem from,' his master asked in a measured tone.

'Some people say that Arillon is the aggressor and others say it is the influence of Mur,' he answered.

'Interesting, and do they speak of the aggression that foments against Arillon from the Southern Kingdoms?'

'They say that they are only intent on restoring order and bringing peace to the three Kingdoms,' said Jeb.

'Really, and who do they say should rule in Arillon in order to maintain this peace?'

'I do not know m' lord but I have heard of the prophecy that tells of the house of Arillon ruling above all others and bringing prosperity once again to Alton Savia,' he answered simply.

'Ah and what if it is King Dragar that will bring about this prosperity?' His gaze levelled at Jeb making him feel uncomfortable once again.

'I am unsure m' lord. There are many voices, who speak about King Dragar,' he faltered, trying to seek an answer he could not settle upon.

'What do you believe boy?' asked his master.

'I believe King Dragar does his best for Arillon,' he lied.

'Well that is good because you are going to meet your king very soon,' said Lord Tarrant, making Jeb's stomach turn in shock.

'Why m' lord?' he asked as his cheeks paled. He had heard about the king and his raging temper from many within the castle and the prospect of meeting him made him very nervous.

'Do not question the will of the king!' Tarrant's voice boomed. Jeb acquiesced and the lesson continued as usual with

Tarrant asking many questions. He was testing Jeb about all the skills needed to be a successful scout and then went on to lecture him about how to be a good ranger. He then told Jeb that the king would be interrogating him later in the day and that it was important that he learn how to relay his instructions to the best of his abilities. They looked at maps of Arillon and Jeb had to learn about the geography that surrounded them and all the important landmarks and way posts. He had to memorise a particular route, which led from Calavaria up into the foothills of the Drakenstein. Tarrant quizzed him on this repeatedly until he remembered it perfectly.

'You are ready to meet your king,' said Lord Tarrant when they had reached a particular juncture in the lesson that coincided with the afternoon chiming of the castle bells. 'King Dragar awaits and we should not keep him waiting,' he continued, digging his long bony fingers into Jeb's shoulder and steering him from the chamber. He guided Jeb along many passages at a breakneck pace until they finally reached the entrance to the throne room. The attending men-at-arms moved aside as Tarrant sailed past with his pawn ahead of him.

'His eminence the Lord Tarrant,' announced the court crier as they entered the great hall. The room was vast and practically empty save for an enormously intricate gold throne at the far end that sat above a short flight of stark, white, marble stairs. Jeb looked up at the vaulted ceilings high above festooned with mosaics depicting heroic figures in battle. The colours of Arillon draped the walls, with the green and gold fabric catching the light from a hundred candelabra flanking the approach to the throne. Sitting with his legs outstretched and his bejewelled hand supporting a bearded chin, the king of Arillon stared at them with vacant, sallow eyes.

'At last,' he said, registering their arrival, 'the little messenger arrives.'

'Yes, here he is my Liege, our little treasure,' followed Tarrant.

'He has been instructed and conditioned accordingly?' the king asked, shifting his gaze to his prelate.

'Yes my Liege. He has proved to be a willing and pliable conduit for our purpose.'

'Well my young scout, you are to be sent on a very special errand that is of the utmost importance to this court. It is very important that you follow my instructions to the letter. Do you understand waif?'

'Yes m' lord,' Jeb answered without a thought. He could not believe that he was now standing before the king of Arillon and that his services were required in this way.

'Good. That is very good. You have memorised the route to take into the foothills of yonder mountains?' He pointed in the direction of the windows beyond which the Drakenstein ranged in the distance. Jeb looked out at the mountains and nodded his head.

'He has a good understanding of the terrain my Liege,' said Tarrant, pushing Jeb closer to the throne.

'Good, most pleasing, you are to carry a message for me into the Sacred Wood. When you arrive at the designated area that Lord Tarrant has revealed to you, you are to find the king's marquee and ask for the bearer of the stone. Do you understand?'

'Yes m' lord,' he answered.

'You are to relay my message to the bearer of the stone alone and nobody else; is that understood?'

'Yes m' lord. Apologies m' lord but what is the message?' he asked, uncertainly.

'Ah yes, the message,' he said with absent-minded measure as he looked out at the horizon, 'do not concern yourself with that now. Lord Tarrant here has already equipped you with all you need for your mission, even though you may not be aware of it yet. In time you will understand and all will be unveiled to bring forth the message which lies within you yet.' He burst into wild laughter, startling Jeb.

Eventually the audience was over and his master permitted Jeb to take his lunch with the other boys before the afternoon lessons in hand-to-hand combat began with Shram. He could not wait to see Oonagh to enquire about the others who came here with him. He was the first to arrive at the kitchen and thought that now was the best time.

'You are early me lad,' Oonagh said, cheerily.

'Yes, had my private lessons again today,' he responded. He looked around to make sure nobody was listening and asked, 'Oonagh do you mind if I ask you something?'

'What is it me lad?' She looked at him quizzically as she went about her preparations.

'What has become of my friends? I have not seen any of them in many days and I am concerned for them.' He blinked and looked up at her imploringly.

'I am not permitted to speak of these things,' she said, her tone changing instantly from one of frivolity to one of caution.

'What things Oonagh, what do you mean?'

'Do not ask of these things my son,' she whispered taking him by the hand and pulling him aside. 'You are going to get us both into a lot of trouble. A lot has changed here in Calavaria since the return of Lord Tarrant. The walls have grown ears in these dark times!'

Jeb looked about at the walls and then at her and back to the walls again. 'I don't get your meaning. Do you mean there are spies?'

'There is much that happens that cannot be explained within these walls. Certain things are best left alone.' There was finality to her statement.

'I see, but does this mean my friends are in danger?' He asked earnestly. 'Please you have to tell me, it is important to me.'

Oonagh sighed and looked at him with sad eyes. 'I do not know my son, all I can say is that they are being sent away one by one, to what ends I cannot tell and dare not ask. Many children are being held in the dungeons.'

'But how do you know this?'

'Because I am responsible for feeding them and when I go down there I notice that their number shrinks by one each week,' she answered under her breath.

'Have you seen Sara?' he asked quickly.

'Yes she is still there,' her eyes darted from left to right taking in the doors and passages behind him. 'That is enough. I have said too much already!'

The other apprentices began filing into the kitchen and interrupted their conversation, making a noise as usual, their voices heightened with excitement about the day's events. Jeb moved to his usual position between two boys he did not much care for.

'What is it?' asked Orrick, a large oaf who irritated Jeb, with a mock look of concern on his face. Orrick had noticed Jeb's expression. Jeb was thinking about the plight of his young friends and the news that Sara was still down below them, in the damp cold somewhere.

'Nothing,' said Jeb, forcing a smile.

'Oh he must be missing his Mummy,' said another boy nearby who had heard them. Without notice Jeb jumped up and punched the lad full square in the mouth. He felt the lip split under his knuckles and watched in detached fascination as the blood trickled over the boy's chin and onto his tunic. Jeb's victim recoiled in shock holding his jaw and fell jabbering to the floor beside the bench like an injured gibbon. One of the wards came over in a flash as the boy stammered, pointing at Jeb, 'he hit me!'

'What is going on here?' shouted the stocky and rather unpleasant looking ward as he stooped over them.

'He hit me,' said the boy again. The others were deathly silent, as they knew the punishment for disorderly behaviour was severe.

'Come with me you scoundrel,' rasped the man as he grabbed Jeb by the shoulders and lifted him out of his seat. Jeb did not put up a fight and went quietly with his captor, looking back over his shoulder as Oonagh wiped his bleeding antagonist's face. He felt a small sense of victory in his mother's honour and smiled inwardly as the ward led him away.

His subjugator threw into a small cell with only dirt on the cold stone floor. The man locked and chained the wrought iron gate and it reminded Jeb of their arrival a few weeks back, when he and the other children found themselves locked in the catacombs. This was the dungeon level and he peered out of his cell, trying to make sense of his surroundings. The sound of dripping water reached his ears and he could not see any of the children anywhere as all the other cells within view were empty. It was dark and a chill wind whistled through the tunnels. He sat reflecting upon his fate for hours before he finally heard some movement nearby. It was the sound of footsteps and next he noticed the flickering orange of torch flame across the walls around him.

'Here he is m' lord,' said a foreign voice.

'Ah, my young apprentice,' chided Lord Tarrant, 'you have been up to no good I hear.' He stood in front of Jeb now in a long, dark red robe with a strange looking headpiece on top of his bald head. 'Well you have actually saved me some trouble by finding your way down here. I was soon to bring you down to these parts for one of your final lessons; but no time like the present.'

Jeb once again felt a sense of dread that he had become accustomed to in his master's presence. His head swam and he felt tired and heavy.

'Come with me boy,' Tarrant's voice boomed.

'Yes m' lord,' he felt himself saying although this was not what he meant to say at all. He meant to ask where they were going and where all the other children were. The gate was unlocked and opened and he stepped out as two armed guards immediately flanked him. They looked different to the regular castle guard. They were very tall and wore dark leather and metal armour from head to foot. He looked up at their faces, hidden by awful looking masks that made him shudder. It was then that he realised that they were Murian. There was a torch and key bearer in front of the party who was also Murian.

Jeb was marched through the dungeons and down into the catacombs along the route that had first brought him here. They descended ever further, with nothing said between them until eventually they arrived at the underground chasm that housed the subterranean lake.

'Here we are finally,' said Tarrant, smiling grimly in the green light of the glowing stalactites that hung above them. 'We are here to witness the strength and wonder of our new alliance and to worship the vessel of our mighty authority. We have brought forth our champion from the depths of Mur. Let this be a lesson to you young scout so that you do not forget your mission or sway from your path. If you do not reach your mark there will be much worse to follow, to your eternal regret.'

Jeb did not quite understand what he meant but looked on with interest. His master's next utterance filled Jeb with horror.

'Bring forth the sacrificial offering.' Tarrant raised his arms to reveal a long silver flute hidden in his robes. One of the guards strode over and began to crank a large wheel to release a massive chain that clamoured to life. A series of pulleys sprang into action and Jeb was aware of movement overhead. He had to blink twice as he could not believe what he was witnessing. A metal cage rattled into view and then swung into place above the dark water. Tarrant held up his hand signalling for the contraption to stop. It was only then that Jeb realised what it was that the small metal cage held.

It was Johnny!

Jeb wanted to scream but found that he had no control over his vocal chords. His throat had closed in fright and it felt as if his legs had turned to lead. His feet seemed cemented in position, unable to move and the small, inert form before him transfixed Jeb. The prelate raised his flute and played a melancholic tune that echoed through the caves with an eerie resonance.

At first there was a ripple on the water's surface lapping gently on the stones at their feet. The ripples turned to crashing waves as the water began to bubble and boil and then, to Jeb's abject terror, a gargantuan beast reared its head clear of the water to tower above them. It had the body of a gigantic snake, the likes of which Jeb had never seen, with black scales that glistened as the writhing tail thrashed in arching coils behind it. The head was hideous in its complexity with a protruding snout above rows of flashing fangs. The eyes glowed red with a piercing gaze that made Jeb's heart skip a beat and bat-like wings flapped frantically behind a mane of spikes.

'Behold Krillafax the amphithere of Mur,' sang Tarrant. 'We offer this soul up to you, our servant of death.' He dropped his arm as a signal to the guard at the wheel who responded by pulling on a lever.

There was a creak and a groan as the bottom of the cage swung open to release the contents. Johnny fell from his tethered prison and a chilling scream echoed through the cavern, as he appeared to come to his senses. Before he hit the water, the serpent-like creature struck through the air with lightening speed to catch the boy in its jaws. With two mind-numbing snaps, Johnny disappeared down the throat of the beast. The last thing Jeb saw was a spray of crimson that spattered across the water to land on Jeb and the sand around him. The world went instantly dark and silent as he lost consciousness.

FIFTEEN

ARRIVAL AT RAVENCROFT

It was late afternoon by the time Dorian and his companions reached the edge of the forest. The fir trees and spruce became sparse and their path began to meander through rolling hills. For the first time they could see the sky as it opened above them displaying low hung clouds like massive grey sails billowing in the wind. The clouds rumbled overhead from dark centres etched with tinges of green and yellow.

'It looks like thundersnow,' remarked Drake.

'I think you may be right there, looks like a typical blasted mountain storm brewing,' agreed Wurt.

No sooner had they spoken than the first snowflakes began to gently flutter down around them. Dorian brushed some from his brow and nose as they landed wet and cold. 'Do we have much further to go?' he asked, trying not to sound like his whining cousin back home.

'Not too far now,' answered Drake, 'another league or two. I think we should make it before this snowfall becomes a problem. These Regan snowstorms are renowned for their ferocity.' He had taken Flynn back onto his own horse a few hours before and looked back to ensure his brother was properly covered. Dorian noticed the concern in his eyes.

The snow began to fall heavily around them, transforming the landscape into a silent, white wilderness. They toiled uphill again and then down, on and on. The wind picked up, swirling the snow around them, making them shiver in their saddles. The sun bowed out in the west and nightfall crept swiftly across the land from the east. As they broke over the next verge, they saw the lights of Ravencroft up ahead in the distance. Yellow light poured out from high turret windows through the relentless blizzard, like beacons to lead the way.

Ravencroft was an elegant, stone keep perched atop a steep hill that reared its head precariously at the very edge of the Sacred Wood. Tall towers of gleaming stone stood side by side, capped by pitched slate roofs like tall warriors in the darkening Regan sky. They quickened their pace towards the beckoning comfort of the warm lights high above them.

'Ravencroft at last,' shouted Drake. His voice was barely audible above the howling wind.

'Now there is a welcome sight for a . . .' Wurt was saying, but the wind snatched the sentence from his mouth and flung it to the heights of the now barely visible edifice before them. Loud thunder boomed overhead and the heavens tormented them with sheets of snow and ice.

They began to ascend the narrow road that wound around the hill at an incredibly steep angle, reminding Dorian of the keep back in Graven. This was even steeper and actually went right the way around the hill, bringing them back to the side of their approach as they spiralled upwards.

Eventually they stood exhausted before enormous gates covered in metal plate. The metal was freezing to the touch as Dorian leant against the gates while dismounting. The journey obviously wore Fire out as his head hung low and his breathing heavy.

'Who goes there?' cried a voice from above.

'Drake Arvin and company,' was the rapid reply.

A few moments later a panel in one of the great doors opened at head height revealing two eyes that peered out from below a silver helmet.

'Show your seal!' demanded the guard.

'Come now Rumbard,' protested Drake, 'we are frozen to the bone.'

'Your seal!'

With a sigh, Drake fumbled inside his cloak and produced an engraved metal seal strung on a thick chain that he wore about his neck. He held it up to the intent eyes.

'Enter,' was the order as the panel snapped shut.

'He takes his job too seriously,' Wurt chuckled.

'I suppose he must in these diabolical times,' noted Drake.

The gates opened with a rattling of chains and a whining of pulleys and before they knew it, they were within the walls and out of the tempest that raged beyond.

The weary travellers found themselves in a long narrow courtyard, brightly lit by torches dotted around the walls. These rose to a great height on all sides and Dorian realised that far above they were open to the blizzard. Snow drifted down around them, some evaporating in the torchlight, most of it making it to the cobbled hay-strewn floor. On the left, he could see numerous dark recesses that led into the depths of the keep and to the right, the stables. Many horses stomped and brayed above the whistling wind, high above. A handful of guards and servants gathered around them to tend to the horses and lower Flynn gently from the saddle. However, the figure descending a staircase into the courtyard directly before them, now held Dorian's attention.

Morgan was a tall, thin man wearing a dark blue hooded cloak with silver trim. The hood covered his head and his arms lay folded together within the sleeves of his robe. As he approached, he unfolded his arms and exposed long slender fingers to draw back his hood. Dorian noticed a ring on each hand sparkling in the ambient light but this was nothing in comparison to the glittering glass beads that adorned his long, snow-white braids and plaited beard. Dorian recognised the stones in his rings as precious and very valuable.

Just then, he felt warmth in the Tamulus and he was almost sure he saw a glowing light in each of the stones in the old man's rings. It was almost as if Morgan's stones had sprung to life on reaching such close proximity to the stone in Dorian's amulet.

'Welcome to Ravencroft men,' the tall man said calmly.

Dorian stared at his thin smiling face, lined with age, but his eyes fascinated him most. They looked so bright and clear, like the eyes of a young man, trapped in an aging body.

'I am Morgan,' he said, bowing slightly.

'I am Dorian.'

'I know,' was the simple response.

Morgan noticed Flynn lying on the ground behind them and his eyes flashed with concern. 'Forgive me,' he said as he brushed past Dorian to examine the ailing soldier. 'Take him to my chambers immediately.' He ordered a group of attendants to promptly lift Flynn up and carry him towards the stairs. Looking at the newcomers he said, 'you must be hungry and you need to bathe.' He looked at Wurt as he said this, the Regan wishing he could melt into the ground. 'Follow Gareth here, he will show you to your quarters where you can bathe and rest. He will send for you in due course for a hot meal, when we shall talk further. Drake, I think you should come with me.'

With that, he hurried away after the receding group of servants, Drake by his side. They spoke in earnest as they went.

'Follow me Sirs,' beckoned Gareth as he led them away through an arch. Gareth led them into one of the dark recesses where he lit a torch. They then followed him into a damp and cold tunnel. They began to ascend first one flight of winding stairs and then another. Dorian thought he might never find his way back. All he could see was the torch up ahead, bobbing and weaving, as Gareth led the way higher into the keep. The torchlight played on the walls between the supporting beams casting elongated shadows at oblique angles and creating an eerie atmosphere. The banners of Ravencroft hung from wall and beam and Dorian was glad when they finally stopped at a small, arched, reinforced door.

'Here we are sirs,' said the torchbearer as he opened the door and stooped into the room beyond.

Inside they found a large room with an iron stove in the corner, pregnant with glowing coals. Four comfortable beds stood parallel completing the furnishings. An inter-leading door gave into a smaller room where two large metal baths stood on ball and claw above a stone tray containing glowing coals. Fragrant steam rose from the baths and Dorian was immediately reminded of a summer glen, abundant with lavender and springy, green grass.

'I shall call for you in one hour,' said Gareth leaving them in peace to disrobe and bathe.

They wasted no time getting out of their cold, damp clothes and hopping into the baths.

'What a relief to get out of those bloodied clothes,' said Wurt, jovially as he glanced over at Dorian in the next tub.

'Yes, Daisy was not the only one to turn her nose up at you,' replied Dorian, smiling as he felt his aching muscles relax. He looked down at his naked body, his eyes resting on the Tamulus. It made him feel safe and at peace, here in this place. He dozed off in the soothing, aromatic, warm water.

'Time to get out;' it was Wurt standing before him fully clothed, 'you have been in there for half an hour. Here is a towel and some fresh clothes.'

Dorian could not believe that he had fallen asleep so easily. He dressed in the tunic and cloak provided. The cloak bore the black and red emblem of a shield and a raven. These colours of Ravencroft were visible throughout the keep. He did not remember ever seeing this motif in any of his history lessons with Miss Lambourne; perhaps it was a secret society.

They lay on the beds discussing the day's events and the imminent hot meal. Dorian's stomach began to protest as they imagined all kinds of delicacies served on silver platters. When they heard a rap at the door, they both jumped up like two ravenous children.

Gareth had come to lead them through to the dining hall. Dorian was famished and thought he might faint if he did not eat soon. They arrived at a large room where many men wearing the mark of Ravencroft sat in rows on low solid benches at about a dozen tables. The flickering curiosity in their eyes made Dorian feel uncomfortable as he entered. He could barely make out their faces above the short, thick candlesticks that lit the tables. The ceiling was low-slung and he had to bow his head so as not to bump his forehead on the dark supporting beams that ran the length of the mess hall. There was a murmur among the men as Dorian and Wurt filed past.

'Over here,' Drake spoke, beckoning them to join him at the other end of the expanse.

'How is Flynn?' asked Dorian as he sat down at the table.

'Still unconscious, although Morgan is taking good care of him,' he said. 'You must be ravenous by now.'

'We are,' answered Wurt, 'I could eat a mountain.'

'You would find that rather difficult,' countered Drake.

'Well a boar or two will do,' shouted Wurt sporting a toothy grin.

Servants served the dinner and the room was abuzz with talk of war and all kinds of strange tidings. The newcomers ate mostly in silence, Dorian wolfing his food down to the astonishment of those around him.

'You'd swear he had never eaten a cooked meal before,' taunted Wurt, patting Dorian hard on the back. He nearly choked and they all laughed raucously.

When they calmed down Drake took on a more serious tone, 'Morgan has called for us at first light, we must rest after dinner. There is a lot to be done on the morrow.'

'Will he not be joining us?' asked Dorian, hopefully.

'Not tonight,' answered Drake, 'he has a formidable task ahead of him. Flynn is in a bad way . . . the damage caused by the Blackwraith and its exorcism is considerable.'

'Will he be alright?' inquired Wurt.

'He is in capable hands. This is a trying time for Morgan, but his powers are great and this night will be the turning point,' answered Drake, gravely.

They finished their meal whilst discussing the dangers they had faced over the past few days. They kept their voices low so as not to draw too much attention to themselves. Dorian could not believe how at home he felt in the company of these men whom he hardly knew. It was as if he had come home to a place that he belonged. He thought about his life in Graven, how he had spent many hours up on the cliffs longing for adventure, and all the sights and sounds of places he had dreamt of. Now, here he was, his destiny inextricably entwined with that of these men, with all the men in this room for that matter. He touched the Tamulus as it lay beneath his shirt and pondered its significance. He knew that there was something mystical about it and that his union with it was but the beginning of some endeavour hereto unfathomable. A bout of laughter that broke out at the table next to theirs drew him out of his reverie. Someone was making fun of one of the more intoxicated soldiers who had fallen over backwards and lay on the floor looking rather un-amused at his compatriots. Before long, they all yawned and decided it would be wise to retire for the night. Drake led them out of the noisy dining hall and through the long, dark passages of the keep to their room.

On reaching their quarters, they took off their boots and summarily flopped onto their beds, their bellies full and the aches and pains of the past couple of days extinct in their muscles. Where Dorian lay he could see through the small window at the foot of his bed, and he watched the snow swirling outside, creating translucent changing shapes that peeked in at him and then passed like phantoms in the night. He drifted off to sleep only to be woken about an hour later by one of the open shutters that had worked itself free on the outside, banging noisily against the wall. He decided to get up and fasten it closed. He opened the window by sliding up the latch and caught the offending board, fastening it down. He had to lean out to reach the other as it had now swung open and as he did so something caught his eye. High up in one of the tallest towers ranging around him he saw a faint blue light glowing from one of the windows. He sensed heat and life in the Tamulus and clasped it in his cold hands. It was with this image in his mind and the warmth at his chest that he finally lay down and fell into a deep slumber, undisturbed by either sound or dream.

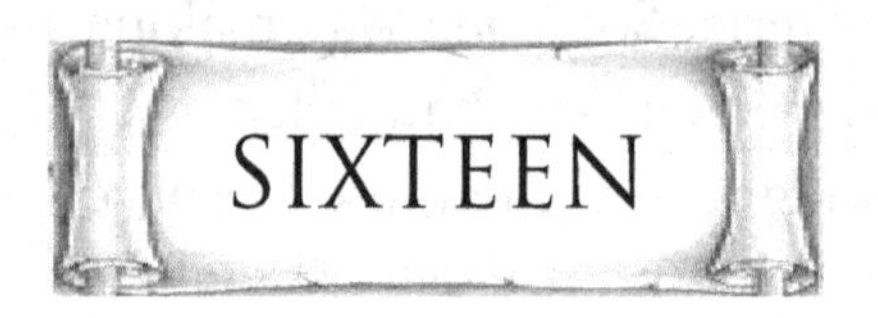

THE BROTHERHOOD OF GUARDIANS

Morgan stood at the window staring out at the relentless blizzard. At first light, he had summoned Dorian, Drake, and Wurt to his chambers in the tallest tower in the keep. Dorian saw that Drake was already here and he imagined that this was where he had witnessed the strange illuminations of the night before. He wondered if it might be the same window.

'Yet again winter torments us from without with her icy breath,' Morgan was saying. He turned to them, looking tired and worn, as if he had run a race through the night. 'There is much to discuss . . . these are desperate times and desperate times call for measures of the same import. The scrimmage between the forces of good and evil once again draw Alton Savia into the fray. We cannot stand by any longer and allow a deluge of pain and suffering to sweep our beloved realm away. It is a time of prophecy and reckoning.' He looked directly at Dorian and paused for a moment, his gaze conveying a sense of deep thought. 'The time has come for the sleeper to awaken.' He said this quietly, almost to himself, as if he was preoccupied with his own thoughts.

'What do you mean?' asked Dorian, feeling a little perturbed.

The others in the room looked at each other and shifted in their chairs, expectantly as if an uncomfortable truth was about to be revealed.

'You are the fulcrum,' said Morgan, moving closer and holding up his fist inferring a foreboding power.

'Me?'

'Your destiny has been preordained, even though you are not aware of it.'

'With all due respect my lord, I am not sure I follow,' said Dorian, feeling rather bewildered yet again.

Morgan walked over to a large teak chest covered in strange carved designs and inlaid with various kinds of metal. He unlocked it and withdrew a large tome. He placed this on the table in the centre of the room and sat down before it.

A reverent silence settled upon the gathered companions and all looked on in anticipation as Morgan unfastened the gleaming leather cover.

'This is the Book of Prophecy,' he said emphatically, 'it has been handed down from one Guardian to the other and dates back many generations, to a time when men first set foot in this land. It contains the writings of kings and seers, of peasants and magicians, of anybody that has been touched by the Wielding and who has had cause to write in it.'

Dorian stared at the book in awe and felt the familiar strange sensation ripple through his body. He knew the feeling came from the Tamulus and it radiated from it like a current to the very tips of his fingers and toes, over his scalp and back again in a continuous cycle. 'What does it say?' he asked, swallowing nervously.

'I shall read some to you . . . this first part dates back to the very beginning and no-one is quite sure who wrote it. It is written in the old tongue, but I shall translate . . .

From the Legend of the Bloodstone

In the beginning two great Nations rose up
One to the North and the Other to the South
And two great Houses Ruled the World.
And their Power was Immense and far reaching
Two Races and Two Kings
Each intent on consuming the other
And their armies were pitted against each other
In battle after battle and countless died
And the Southern King summoned his greatest Magician
Ordering him to create a Weapon that would smite his
Enemy from the face of the World

And the Mage known as Borratar dwelt in the
Northern Wilderness and bore from the Mountains
The Obsidian Mask
His King rode into battle wielding the power of the Mask
And destroyed the North murdering their King
And he ruled the known World with an Iron fist for a
Thousand years

'This was a dark period in our history,' said Morgan, 'when most of the known world's population lived in fear and oppression. For generations Borratar's evil creation was used by the cruel kingdom to subdue all that might attempt to rise up against it.'

'That bastard Borratar met with a gruesome end, not soon enough I say,' blurted Wurt, hardly able to contain himself. He had been sitting on the edge of his seat, eyes wide, like a child hanging on every word.

'What happened to him?' asked Dorian consumed with keen interest.

'I shall continue . . .

The will of the underdog was strong
And the family that was seemingly once destroyed
Arose again in secrecy
A new King gathered strength and a following
That vowed to place him once again in his rightful place
Upon the throne of Arillon

A powerful brotherhood was formed
And they set out to find a way to overcome
The curse of the Obsidian mask
The King in waiting sent forth his magicians
To find the thing that would crush the South
And so it was that the Earth-Mother gave up
The Bloodstone into the hands of Arillon

A red stone infused with the knowledge
And power of aeons
Finally came to rest in the crown of the new King
And he rode forth leading the North into battle with the South once again

Morgan looked up and his eyes met Dorian's eyes. A strange rumination lay there that Dorian could not fathom. 'Well did he win the battle against the south?' asked Dorian as he shuffled his feet distractedly.

'He certainly did!' interjected Wurt unable to resist.

Drake who had been unassuming until now, apart from a courteous nod when they came in, said 'Let him finish Wurt.'

Morgan smiled for a moment and then resumed:

And the Great battle raged for eleven days and nights
And the Northern King smote his enemy from the face of the earth

In the final throes of Death, the King of the South tried to
Wield All of his power through the Obsidian Mask
With Borratar and his evil serpent slaves at his side
And the Powers
Of good and evil were pitched at each other

And there was a blinding light
And the Earth was split asunder
And so too was the Bloodstone as it gave up its final
Emanation as the Whole Stone

'What happened to it?' asked Dorian.

'It was broke in two,' cried Wurt, totally unable to contain himself any longer. He jumped up and pointing at Dorian's chest he shouted, 'you've got half of it there in the Tamulus!'

'Half of it,' said Dorian, 'well what happened to the other half then?'

'It was forged into the hilt of a great sword known as *Disparager*,' said Morgan.

As he said this name, it hung in the air with a dull resonance above the heads of the gathered men. Beneath everyone sat silently in wonderment of the name.

'*Disparager* and the *Tamulus* have been in the hands of the house of Arillon for centuries. Generations of Kings have borne it out across the battlefields of Alton Savia, crushing their foe or any who dared to stand in their path. However, for the last three hundred years the lords of the North and South have been living in peace. It was decided that the great sword of Kings be hidden in a place of safety many years ago, to keep it out of hands that may try to wield its power for their own selfish ends,' said Morgan. 'Though the sword is now hidden from us, there is one who knows where it lies, we need to retrieve it and bring it back into the light of day and the world of Men,' Morgan continued. 'It was the mountain men of Rega who were entrusted to hide and protect the sword, and now their secret lies solely with the Oracle at Dorne. You must seek her out in the mountains of Rega. The true might of Arillon can only be realised once again through the reunion of the two parts of the Bloodstone.'

'Many tales are told in Rega of its whereabouts. Some say it was given to a dragon for safekeeping and there is a fable in that too that I heard as a boy,' said Wurt, leaning forward eagerly.

'So we need to find the sword and do what with it?' asked Dorian, his brow wrinkled.

'The current king of Arillon's claim to the throne is false,' Drake responded. 'King Dragar is the bastard half-brother of Good King Gordon, who was poisoned roughly two decades back. King Gordon's queen had his first-born child stolen away into hiding at birth in fear for its life. It was not long before she too was murdered. Dragar claimed the throne as the next in line of succession and now, rumour has it, that he leans to the Dark Order. He too seeks the sword to wield it to his own ends. There are still those in his court who suspect his hand in the deaths of the king and queen. Their spies talk of a secret alliance between the Empress of Mur and the beleaguered king's army of Arillon.' Everyone put their fists to their chests in the customary salute of respect at the loss of the much-loved King Gordon.

'So it is left to the true living heir to the throne of Arillon. For only he can find *Disparager* and wield its power once again,' said Morgan, looking deep into Dorian's soul. He turned to the tome once more and said, 'I shall read from the new book of prophecy . . .'

And it shall come to pass
That the world will once again
Find itself in the clutches of Evil
And brother shall rise against brother
And the Golden Throne shall be possessed by Demons
But the fruit of the true King shall rise
And make the Bloodstone whole again
To vanquish the slain and bring peace and prosperity where there is suffering and pain

'So it is that we come to be in the service of the prince of Arillon, son of Gordon and true heir to the throne in Calavaria,' said Drake. 'It is *you* Prince Dorian.'

'What,' exclaimed Dorian, 'you must be insane?'

'No my lord,' continued Drake, 'you are indeed the one true heir to your father's throne. You know this deep within your heart. Think on it for a while and you will know it to be true.'

Dorian looked at the floor, stunned. He reflected on this earth-shattering news for a moment. Slowly the realisation that everything he had heard could indeed be true dawned on him. Drake was right; he had somehow always known these things deep down inside and yet not in the forefront of his mind. It was like an amazing secret unveiled by a great magician, where the outcome was suspected but the design of its origin a mystery.

His mind reeled as he tried to focus on the enormity of the challenge before him as this truth crystallized. Strangely, all he could see in his mind's eye was Toby's expression on hearing this news, with one eye searching disbelievingly, in vain, for a different truth. He smiled.

'What now my lord?' asked Dorian, 'what are we to do next?' His voice faltered as he asked this question and he looked at the others with a sadness that was beyond his years.

'You must swear allegiance to the Brotherhood and then embark on a quest to find Disparager before Dragar does. Once you have the whole stone in your possession, you will be in a position to overthrow the usurper Dragar and claim your rightful seat in the Kingdom of Arillon,' said Morgan. 'The time has come for you to enter the golden halls of Calavaria, your true home and the seat of power in *your* troubled kingdom. It will be a dangerous quest and we do not want the evil prying eyes of Mur to discover you. Indeed, secrecy is paramount and men will have to be spirited through the lands with stealth. There must be haste and silence.'

'I agree my lord,' said Drake, 'silence in the black of night and the speed of the wind. I once served your father King Gordon.' He looked at Dorian and there was a look of remorse in his eyes. 'You now have the protection of my sword.'

'And the protection of my bow,' added Wurt.

'I would expect nothing less from members of our Brotherhood,' said Morgan.

'What of Flynn my lord?' asked Drake.

'Ah yes. Flynn lies between the world of men and that of the nether spirits. I have borne him from the danger of Death's grasp as best I could. He will need Mia's blessing and many days of rest. I am certain that he will be ready to follow the Voltarian contingent before long,' answered Morgan, 'he will travel with me and my guard when we leave for Caledon to join our allies.'

'The king of Voltar has agreed to dispatch his army?' asked Drake.

'Yes, I held council with him just days ago and he is aware of the pending danger to the Alliance. I received word that he too is aware of how imminent this threat is. A massive mobilisation from both Voltar and Rega is taking place as we speak,' responded Morgan, with a grave face. 'I await word from Regavik. We are to follow King Mogador's army east through Rega and pass through Hoth's Gate in the Drakenstein to the plains of Caledon. There we will meet King William's men and the forces that have risen in secret against Dragar. From there we will head for Calavaria to face and defeat the guard of Arillon still faithful to Dragar. You must take the boy and a small team and head for the Oracle, through the mountains to the north-west. We will prepare the horses for you, pack lightly,' he added, 'you leave at dusk. The cover of darkness will be of great benefit. You and Wurt know these mountains like a child its own back yard.'

'Aye, that is true,' said Wurt grinning. 'They will not spy us!'

'I will hold council with Dorian in private before you leave,' said Morgan. 'I will instruct him as best I can with regard to the Wielding, amongst other things and then we will welcome him into our secret circle as a true defender of our sovereignty.'

THE WIELDING

Morgan spent two days instructing Dorian in many things relating to the state of the three Kingdoms. The Brotherhood sheltered within Ravencroft went about preparations for battle. On the third afternoon, as the prevailing storm outside gathered strength and ripped the hoarfrost from the trees throwing up white columns at their stony mountain retreat, Dorian found himself in yet another chamber within the fortress. The room reminded him very much of the apothecary in Graven, however, in comparison the Graven apothecary appeared small and empty. Here row upon row of bottles and vials lined the shelves and Dorian investigated them in an attempt to discover their contents languishing in murky suspensions. He stopped to examine one in particular more closely. He tilted the glass allowing the bobbing object to roll forward until it touched the side. He recoiled in fright; it was a human eye!

'Ah yes, old Grey,' said Morgan.

'Who was that?' asked Dorian, returning the bottle to its original position. Dorian looked over at Morgan and saw the amusement in his eyes.

'You mean who *is* that. His eye is still with us and links our two worlds. That of the Dead and ours,' answered Morgan with a smile that made Dorian feel like a naughty child caught in the act of stealing a sugary tart.

'My lord?'

'He is one of my predecessors, Aaron the Grey, a guardian and great Captain of the Brotherhood. He is keeping an eye on things here in Ravencroft.'

"Morgan's smile makes a mockery," thought Dorian. 'Surely you jest,' he said, 'it is not really looking at us is it?' He felt uncomfortable and took a step backwards.

'There are many things you do not yet comprehend,' said Morgan, the smile gone now.

'Yes, so much has happened in such a short space of time. It all feels like a dream that has become real.' He looked at Morgan, wistfully twirling a lock of his hair.

'A lot to take in I am sure,' Morgan conceded, his eyes taking Dorian in from head to toe. 'These events would weigh heavily on any man. You are strong though Dorian, very young, but strong. I sense a strong willpower within you, something that you *must* learn to use effectively. The power that Mia offers up to you can be bent to your will.'

'The Tamulus has been doing many strange things,' said Dorian, again aware of the stone beneath his shirt.

'Indeed, it has sprung to life. This portends well for our cause. It has accepted you as true to its bloodline.' There was a note of respect in Morgan's voice.

'It knows me?'

'It knows the blood that flows in your veins and connects you to it and the power that feeds it.'

'What power my lord?' enquired Dorian.

'I think it is time you called me Morgan. It is the power offered up to us by Mia herself,' he answered, his eyes glittered like the many beads, which haloed his face.

'Is this a good power my . . . Morgan?' he corrected.

'It is the force of nature Dorian. It is neither good nor bad. Whoever can wield this power can bend it to their will. If the wielder has dark intentions, his design will be realised through the mechanism of his calling.'

'I always thought there were good and evil forces,' said Dorian.

'Most people do. The truth is that it is not the actual force that is either good or bad but rather the one who summons it.'

'I see, and the mechanism is the stone?' He felt rather pleased with himself for understanding.

'Yes exactly, like the mask or any other portal in existence that may serve as a channel for this power,' Morgan continued. 'It is the will of the bearer that matters.'

'Is the mask tied to the bloodline of its bearer?'

'We do not know. I have not encountered this device and I am not sure how it has been crafted.' He looked out at the white blizzard rattling his window frames as it attempted to gain entry into his warm enclave in the tower. 'She is angry.'

'Who, the witch?' asked Dorian.

Morgan's amusement returned, 'no, Mia.'

'How many Gods are there?' asked Dorian, his mind turning to the stories and lessons he had been privy to over the past few years. He realised the gravity of their situation and it became clear to him how it was that he came to be educated in these matters at all. No other children in his village were educated apart from himself and his cousin. He had never thought this odd before, as his uncle was much better off than anyone else in Graven was. Now he understood that there was a plan to ensure his tutorage, most likely under the auspices of the Baron.

'Many,' Morgan turned his attention to Dorian once more, 'some we know of and many more we do not. Our people have worshipped many Gods through the centuries, but Mia is the one we have the most faith in now. She answers our prayers and has given us the Bloodstone.'

'Is the mask from Mia too?' He felt like a young child asking a million questions.

'I do not think so,' said Morgan, slowly, 'I believe it has been offered up by an elder God, one not of this world.'

'I do not get your meaning my lord,' Dorian was bewildered again.

'They say that when Borratar conjured up this black token in the mountains, it arrived in a ball of fire from the skies.' Morgan folded his hands in front of him on the small table.

'It was a star that fell to Earth then,' stated Dorian, feeling as if he understood what Morgan meant.

'It may well have been.'

'The Tamulus has enabled me to do things,' said Dorian, hoping to get some clarity on these matters.

'What things do you speak of?'

Dorian went on to tell him about the feelings he had encountered back in Graven and the rock fall in the mountains. He also related his visions and most importantly, the encounter with the Blackwraith he had ousted from poor Flynn. Morgan was most interested in this episode and asked him many questions about the nature of the experience.

'My understanding is that the Tamulus has certain powers. It has been known to allow its bearer to access visions of the past and also to sense danger or evil from another who has abilities in these things, but to exorcise a Blackwraith or move rock, this is new to me.' He reflected on these facts for a few moments, falling silent and staring down at his hands. His fingers were interlaced and he turned his hands up now, inspecting his palms.

'What of Disparager?' asked Dorian, after a short silence. As he said this name, he felt a crackle against his skin where the Tamulus hung at his chest. He jumped in consternation. 'It keeps tantalising me.'

'Ha, it awaits the reunion with its counterpart. The two halves brought together make a formidable weapon. Kings have won battles, armies have been destroyed, and castles razed to the ground in the wake of Disparager.'

'What does this sword do?'

'It is not the sword that carries the power Dorian, but rather the stone embedded in its hilt that allows the bearer to channel the wild forces of nature. It is the crimson eye in Disparager that completes the Bloodstone and it is the whole stone that was given to us by Mia to strengthen the bloodline of Arillon.'

'I see, and how do I control these wild forces?'

'That is indeed the question my young prince. We must first get you to control the abilities that the Tamulus has bestowed upon you thus far. It is time for us to concentrate all of our efforts on getting you to master its energies.'

They spent the remainder of the afternoon discussing the Tamulus and how best to bend its powers to Dorian's will. Dorian had to spend hours focussing on the stone with his mind and calling upon its strength. His efforts rewarded him with many visions and a keen awareness of people's intentions within a certain radius. He could sense whether they were good or bad and whether there was any danger about. He sensed no real danger within the confines of Ravencroft but was aware of a lurking malevolence beyond the reaches of the Sacred Wood.

He felt ructions of anger in some of the men nearby but no foreboding.

Morgan taught Dorian how to control his emotions and to hone his skills of perception, all the time using the Tamulus as a guide and measure. Dorian became aware of how it communicated with him and gained an understanding of its past. A particular vision moved him, which came to him in the depths of a meditative trance. His father, King Gordon smiled and reached out to him across a great divide. Their similarity in demeanour struck Dorian and he felt a yearning to embrace the man he had never met. There was an enchanting benevolence about his personage and Dorian wanted to reach out to him. Try as he might, he could never quite touch his father, and his heart ached with longing as he surrendered to the emotion wracking his senses. Dorian had not cried many tears in his life before. He was unfamiliar with what it felt like, but now he wiped his cheek as the salty warmth trickled to the corner of his mouth. Morgan encouraged him to embrace all of these feelings, telling him that he would never be whole and balanced unless he accepted these natural ebbs and flows that Mia bestows upon humanity.

'To harbour one's emotions without surrendering to them, or to imprison those feelings that seek unleashing, leads to illness and regret and can sully a man's judgement,' said Morgan. This lesson was one of many Morgan revealed to his ward during the hours that followed. Morgan was a wise man and Dorian entrusted him with his innermost thoughts and feelings, divulging aspects of himself that he had shared with no other.

By the time they had exhausted all avenues in regards to the arcane knowledge that Morgan could impart, it was dark outside and time for the evening meal. They went down to the great dining hall and sought the counsel of Drake and Wurt and a few other men assigned to their party. As they supped, the conversation turned to the forthcoming journey in search of the Oracle.

'Nobody has seen the Oracle for at least ten years,' Wurt was saying. 'She does not reveal herself so freely these days. The last person that was worthy of her presence was a great Sage in the service of the king of Rega. He sought the wisdom of the Oracle in relation to an illness that had befallen the king's youngest son. He rode for many days and waited many more at Dorne, offering up gifts to the Sacred Wood in order to summon the Oracle. Eventually she appeared only to take his offerings in the name of the forest and to leave him with news he did not appreciate having to take back to an angry king.'

'What did she say,' asked Dorian.

'That the king's son suffered from an incurable malady and that he would die before the next full moon,' Wurt was sombre in his response. He followed this statement by imbibing the entire contents of his large beer tankard and banged it on the table, signalling his wish for a refill. One of the men who had been listening broke into spontaneous laughter but soon curtailed his outburst, thinking better of it, when he saw the look on the fierce little man's face.

'How many days ride to Dorne,' asked Drake, thinking it wise to break the silence and distract Wurt from what was surely to become an exhibition in Regan patriotism.

Wurt turned his attention to Drake, his expression softening somewhat, 'about two days from here.'

'We need to gather offerings for you to place before the Oracle,' said Morgan, 'hopefully we can find something that will take her fancy.' He smiled, intimating that she might be difficult to please.

'What was it that the Oracle accepted from the king's Sage?' asked Dorian.

'Apparently she was quite fond of six of the Kings finest silver chalices. Sparkling gems encrusted them and they were worth a small fortune. A handsome price to pay for news that was already known,' Wurt was scowling again.

'I have a purse of silver coins that was given to me by the Baron of Graven,' offered Dorian. He was feeling hopeful that this might entice the Oracle.

'Indeed, that would be a handsome price for her services; however, I think to be safe we should ensure that you have a wider selection of wares. I will see to it that we gather a few shiny valuables together as these seem to be her preference.' Morgan called one of his aides to their table and went about briefing him on what to do.

'A bit of a magpie really, the old hag is!' Wurt seemed wholly unhappy with the prospect of meeting her.

'We shall ride at first light provided this blizzard breaks,' said Drake, 'I shall ensure that our party is well armed and prepared. I will speak with one of my captains and ask that he select ten of his best men for this mission.' He left the table and Dorian felt a pang of anxiety as he realised what was to come. He dwelt upon the gravity of his situation and whether the Oracle would divulge the hiding place of Disparager.

Morgan stood up and rang a silver bell on the table before him. 'It is time for the induction of our latest member into the Brotherhood of Guardians. Let us light the way for our new disciple.' The room fell silent as the men stood up one by one to light a candle placed before each of them. They left the table and formed a tunnel, two rows of men facing each other, arms arched, and hands touching. A colonnade of candlelight was formed that led from the dining hall into a courtyard lined with the colours of Ravencroft. Dorian's instruction was to pass through the tunnel. At the centre of the courtyard sat an old, stone fountain that gurgled with warm water infused with an herbal concoction. Fragrant steam rose from the water's surface and hung in the air around the gathering like a veil. Morgan moved to the far side of the fountain and said, 'come forward Dorian of Arillon and kneel before your brothers.'

Dorian stepped forward and knelt on a bolster placed before him. 'I am here my lord,' he said.

Morgan drew water from the fountain and wiped Dorian's brow with his wet hands. 'I cleanse you with Mia's water of life,' he chanted. A man then handed him a garland of spruce, birch twigs, and ivy, which he brushed across Dorian's back and arms, placing them in the young prince's hands. 'Repeat after me,' he said, 'In Mia I trust.'

'In Mia I trust.'

'I swear my allegiance to the Brotherhood of Guardians and shall protect the bloodlines of Alton Savia with my life.'

Dorian repeated these words and as he did so, he felt a strange new power within the Tamulus. It was strong and reassuring and images of past kings and heroes forged onwards in his mind. This felt right and just. There was a cry of celebration from the men as soon as he had completed the oath. He was welcomed into their fraternity with many friendly pats on the back and a barrage of forearm clasping, as was the custom.

After the ceremony, the men moved back to the dining hall where they told many stories, which they had heard about the Oracle. Dorian just listened intently, marvelling at this newfound camaraderie. He had many questions about his father for Drake and sat beside him at the first opportunity. They discussed Drake's past service to the House of Arillon at length and Dorian was glad of the time well spent.

The men's voices clamoured around Drake and Dorian who were deep in conversation. They were all very cautious of the weather and contemplated their options in the face of Mia's perpetual assault. Drake told Dorian many stories of his youth in Arillon and of Flynn's dream of joining the army. Flynn had persuaded Drake to enlist when he was merely sixteen and his younger brother followed suit two years later. Drake soon made his mark within the ranks of the infantry and his superiors promoted him to lieutenant by the time he was twenty years old. His prowess as an officer soon reached the ears of the king and before long King Gordon promoted Drake to his private palace guard. Here he grew to respect and love the king and stood at his side through many campaigns and adventures. Upon King Gordon's premature death Drake suspected the foul hand of the king's brother Dragar, escaping soon afterwards with Flynn to seek their fortunes in the mountains of Rega. Here they found Morgan the Free and his band of brothers in arms who had taken up the cudgel against Dragar. Morgan had resurrected the age-old secret society of the Brotherhood whose mantra it was to maintain the sovereignty of the Three Kingdoms.

Eventually, after the singing of a few well-known folksongs that had men clapping and dancing, with their bellies full and their thirst quenched, they found their way to their beds. There was no life in the Tamulus after the festivities and Dorian welcomed the onset of a deep sleep, knowing that they all needed a good rest before embarking upon the quest at hand.

THE NORTHERN TRACK

When Dorian awoke and opened his eyes in the early hours of the following morning, the storm outside had subsided. Everything was deathly quiet apart from the snoring that erupted from Wurt's nasal cavities. The hush outside was what one experienced when the world had been covered in winter's white mantle. Dorian stole out of bed and threw some kindling into the small stove that had lost its heat through the night. Walking over to the window, he peered out at the vast wood that extended in all directions. Thick snow blanketed the trees with the dawn light casting long blue shadows between them. Above, the heavens were clear and the morning star twinkled in the east, heralding the arrival of the sun. Down below he noticed movement as two squirrels scampered about taking advantage of the favourable conditions to forage among some exposed roots.

"A perfect morning for an adventure," he thought to himself. He was feeling excited at the prospect of reaching the Oracle and, hopefully, learning the whereabouts of Disparager. He also felt apprehension at the thought of holding the great sword in his hands and imagined the weight of expectation that would surely come with it. Was he strong enough to face up to the responsibilities so recently cast upon him? "Am I truly the saviour of Arillon?" he asked himself.

'Good morning Sire,' Drake said having awoken too. 'Time to wake that rumbling beast,' he quipped, nodding towards the sleeping dwarf whose toes danced in harmony with his heaving chest. He roused Wurt by shaking his shoulder rather roughly.

'Huh? What the . . .' he was clearly startled and instinctively went for his blade.

'Now, now,' said Drake, 'no need for a scrap! It is time to rise and shake the cobwebs from your ears. The storm has passed and we must away. Let us take breakfast together and see to our horses.'

'It seemed you would sleep forever Wurtel.' Dorian thought it was a perfect moment for jest as the startled dwarf looked at them in dismay.

'You told him,' he bellowed, jumping from his bed to land a heavy heel on Drake's big toe.

'Dorian you shame me,' cried Drake, hopping around in mock anguish.

'It will serve you both well to abstain from using my given name.' Wurt held up his fist in warning.

'I'm sorry, but why do you not like it?' asked Dorian wide eyed, 'I think it is a good strong name.'

'That is only a taste of it,' said Drake, 'it's a good thing I did not divulge the full secret of his lengthy Regan forename.'

'And if you ever do,' Wurt sputtered, 'it will be the last thing you ever say.' The red faced, short man did not look at all impressed and Dorian thought it best to leave it at that, although he was dying to know what this name was.

They gathered their meagre belongings and trundled down to take breakfast in the great hall. Ravencroft was abuzz with men going about the business of preparation for their departure. In the kitchens fires blazed and the aroma of roasting meat made Dorian salivate in anticipation. They met Morgan who was briefing the men who were to accompany their party through the mountains to Dorne. 'Well met gentlemen, and what a fine morning it is to be riding west. I gather you slept comfortably?'

'Indeed my lord, thank you,' said Dorian, 'your hospitality has been most gracious.'

'Sounding like a true king already,' Wurt pulled his belt up with one hand and stroked his beard with the other as he cocked his head at Dorian, his cheeks returning to their usual burnished amber.

'I see you are all in good spirits,' Morgan smiled, 'good, you will need to keep your wits about you in the coming days. Let us break bread together and give thanks to Mia.'

After the prayer the men sat down together to enjoy their meal. Morgan advised them of the best route to take through the mountains. Dorne lay in a valley at least three hundred leagues away on much higher ground. This meant they would need to rest more often so that the animals as well as the men could become accustomed to the thinner, colder air.

Wurt had made this journey a few times before and was confident that the route they had chosen was the best under the current conditions. 'Aye, it may be a bit tricky in places, but I think this would definitely be the best route,' he pointed at a line on the parchment he had spread open on the table in front of them.

'Is this not the territory of the mountain troll?' asked Drake, pointing to a region that lay directly in the path that Wurt had indicated.

'We will skirt the area and hopefully not come across any,' answered Wurt. 'I think we will be pretty safe. We have not had any attacks in this northern region for many years and, in any event, the trolls are hibernating for the winter.'

'Well that is a good thing,' said Dorian, 'I've heard that the Regan trolls in these mountains can be quite dangerous, especially during the winter months if they are disturbed.'

'I have instructed my men to be extra vigilant. They will also be carrying crossbows with poisonous bolts. These are some of my most trusted and skilled rangers and have sworn to guard you with their lives.' The captains who sat with them reinforced Morgan's assurance. They banged their fists on their chests and repeated their oaths.

'In the true king's service,' they chanted.

He felt obliged to say something, 'thank you gentlemen, your service is much appreciated.' He thought that he sounded a little dry and added, 'we shall be steadfast in our quest and woe-betide any who challenge us.'

There was a chorus of approval.

They ate breakfast and the chatter amongst the men reached fever pitch until Morgan finally stood up to wish them well on their way. 'May Mia's presence guard and protect you and the sun light your way with favourable conditions,' he said, 'the time has come for the crowning of the true king of Arillon and the brave men of the Brotherhood must once again safeguard the sovereignty of Alton Savia.' A cheer rose up from the men and Dorian felt a surge of pride well up to match it.

After saying their farewells and gathering their weapons and rations as well as the gifts for the Oracle, the party of three friends and ten rangers left the warmth of Ravencroft to make their way down the hill into the wood. Wurt sat perched atop Daisy once again and Dorian could see she had rested well, as she had a spring in her step. Fire too was full of beans and playfully nipped at Drake's horse Brag. It was as if spring was in the air and yet Dorian knew this to be impossible. The season had not yet reached its climax.

Once they had reached the foot of the hill, it was not long before they entered the wood by the path that Wurt had chosen, taking them towards the northwest. The territory was quite level for the most part. After about two hours, the path narrowed and began to climb between the trees, signalling the ascent into the mountains. There was not much chatter now as they travelled in single file; the track unable to provide purchase for two horses abreast and the riders more inclined to focus on the way ahead. The scout would occasionally shout back information regarding the nature of the terrain.

They travelled this way for most of the day and as they rose higher into the mountains, the temperature dropped steadily. The air became thinner, forcing them to stop occasionally to catch their breath. By late afternoon, they reached a landing between two steep inclines where the trees were less dense. The scout signalled for them to stop as this was the designated area for their evening break. The sky was still clear though a freezing wind howled up the valley and pierced their clothing with unrelenting fervour.

'What an incredible view from here,' said Drake, looking back at the way they had come. Far below them pockets of fog clung to the valleys and they could see a tendril of smoke rise steadily into the heavens, signalling the position of Ravencroft among the snow covered trees.

'Ravencroft seems so far away now,' Wurt piped up as he settled Daisy with a feedbag of millet, 'and still we have far to go.'

'This has been a trying ride. Will it be much the same from this point?' asked Dorian. His back was hurting from the uncomfortable ride through the foothills.

'Yes my lord, we still have a day's hard ride before we reach Dorne,' said Wurt looking at Dorian, 'we shall reach the plateau tomorrow in the rift valley. From there the track is more even.'

'We shall have to set up camp further back between the rocks,' interjected Drake. 'Get the men to unpack as little as possible.' He spoke to the head of the guard who immediately began barking orders to his men. It did not take them long to set up camp as they assembled the bare minimum for shelter and rolled out their beds beneath the makeshift tents. Two men made a small fire and soon they were all huddled between the crags, trying to stay warm as nightfall swiftly approached. As usual, the men spoke of war and what lay ahead of them on the morrow. Night's cold, black fall was sharp and the men had to sleep side by side to keep warm, their blankets being no match for winter at these upper alpine reaches.

Dorian felt warmth in the Tamulus as he drifted into a much-needed sleep. He was stiff all over and could not get comfortable, no matter how hard he tried. The last thing he remembered was a vision of a lake and someone calling out to him from the far side.

It felt like he had merely blinked, for now someone was shaking him awake. He did not want to rise at all and tried to bury himself beneath his cloak and scant covering. 'What, is it morning already?'

'That it is young Sire.' Wurt stood before him, holding out a steaming mug of soup.

'You have been busy.' Dorian smiled and accepted the hot broth appreciatively. The sun was about to rise and overnight;

the sky had filled with heavy cloud. 'That does not bode well for us,' he nodded towards the ominous looking heavens.

'Indeed! Winter's breath may savage us yet again as we ascend even further. This northeastern range can be unforgiving in inclement weather like this. We should make haste and attempt to reach the rift well before nightfall today.'

'Good idea, what does Drake say of this?'

Just then, the man he had come to know and respect over the past days appeared before them, having seen to the horses. 'Say of what?' he asked.

'Wurt was just saying that it would be best if we made haste for the rift valley as that weather looks like trouble.'

'You read my mind Wurt,' he said looking at the little man who sipped on his own hot breakfast.

'From here the path becomes even narrower and I think it will be best if we fasten our ropes between each pair of men,' Wurt looked concerned.

With that, they informed the rest of the party of the strategy and once they had packed up the camp, the men went about fastening themselves one to another in pairs. Some of the men did not like the idea but, after hearing the logic behind it, they realised the potential danger if one of the horses lost its footing and fell from the mountain.

The track became quite treacherous and Dorian found himself looking down a precipice on numerous occasions. He and Drake were tethered and the two horses they rode were very close as they grappled with the rocky track. The situation appeared to annoy Fire and Dorian was certain he would bite Brag's yellow-brown tail as it swished in front of his nose.

It was then that Dorian felt a sharp prick from the Tamulus. It sent ripples through his body and a terrible vision entered his mind. Danger was at hand and it was coming from the skies! While sheltered by the Sacred Wood he had felt nothing, but now as they lay exposed to the elements on the eastern face of the mountain, he sensed something seeking them out. A dark ominous force reached out across the valley and he recognised it as the same entity that had sought him out before. He could see the enormous bat like creatures before they appeared in the skies above them.

'WATCH OUT!' he screamed, 'we are under attack!'

'Where, what is it?' Drake spun around to see Dorian pointing out over the panorama before them at a small black cloud that approached swiftly. 'Take positions,' he shouted to the men, 'there, over there.' He jumped from his horse and pulled him back, dropping to his knee and drawing his crossbow from its cradle on the saddle. His men did the same withdrawing their weapons, some taking cover behind their horses. There was not much cover here and Dorian fell in beside Drake pulling his weapon out on the way down. Fire bucked and let out a whinny, indicating he realised something untoward was afoot. Drake smacked Brag on his rump and sent the horse galloping up the track. Fire did not hesitate and followed suit.

'What is it?' asked Drake.

'The Tamulus has warned me and I have been given a vision. They look like large bats! Ugly ones at that, but they are possessed with an evil presence.'

'Driven by Mur no doubt,' said Drake disgustedly.

'We shall put up a good fight my friends.' Wurt had run up the path. He planted himself on the other side of Dorian. 'They will not get past me,' he said with a large grin on his face and his bow and broadsword at the ready.

'Good man,' said Drake, 'into the fray it is then!' He leant forward and shouted down the line, 'wait for my mark men.'

Within seconds, the dark mass in the sky was above them. It was a colony of bats descending upon them in a crazed attack. These were larger than any bat Dorian had ever seen before. They had large fangs and long claws that cut through the air like daggers, but the strangest thing of all was their long curled tails flapping behind them like snakes.

'What are they?' asked Wurt looking quite perplexed.

'I don't know,' answered Dorian, 'but they want blood!'

'Now,' shouted Drake. On his command, the party of soldiers raised their weapons and loosed their deadly bolts at the incumbent brood. Many found their mark, as the creatures were only paces away now. They shrieked and fell to the ground like stones, some rolling down the mountainside. A few men managed to get a second shot off into the mass of black, flapping wings but now they were attacking in earnest. The men drew their swords and daggers and chopped at their foe with force. Men screamed and shouted as the bats drew blood, and Dorian found himself battling a particularly large monster that bore down on him.

'Look out,' Wurt warned as he drew closer to Dorian in an attempt to aid him in his plight. Dorian had drawn his dagger in one hand and his broadsword in the other after dropping his crossbow and slashed at the creature as it snarled and spat at him. His dagger tore through the beast's chest and he heard an awful sound escape from its throat as it plummeted to earth, spattering him in blood.

Men were hacking away furiously all down the track. Spiked flails spun through the air and Dorian could see blood everywhere now. The ground lay thick with it and it covered his companions like red pitch. It was a horrendous sight and he reeled as the salty stench of bile filled the air. Then, to his dismay, a man fell from the mountain to dangle precariously by his safety rope. That part of the track stuck out from the rest. His companion attempted to rescue him by pulling him up to safety but he too was under attack as three of the creatures went for his unprotected flank. The soldier above lost his footing as the bloodthirsty bats bombarded him and he fell screaming from the ledge dragging his tethered partner to a shared fate.

"This must end," Dorian thought to himself. He felt his anger rise inside of him as it had done in the forest with the Blackwraith. The Tamulus responded, feeling his anger and with a burst of willpower, Dorian projected his anger into the stone, channelling it out towards the winged enemy that surrounded them. A blinding light flashed from the heart of the Bloodstone and eclipsed the menacing swarm as it swirled overhead.

The creatures were dazed and confused as if instantly drunk on some foul liquor. The men saw their chance and immediately went to work destroying them one by one. Their crossbows came out to accompany their swords as the mass literally fell apart before their eyes. Having lost the advantage the hideous bats succumbed to the poisoned bolts and razor sharp steel that cut them down like weeds.

'Are they filled with Blackwraiths?' asked Wurt as he came up to Dorian, sheathing his blood-soaked sword.

'No, I did not sense that they were possessed at all. The power that drives them is far from here and now that they are dead or dying, I do not feel the presence of the evil within them any longer.' He inspected the one at his feet pushing it over with his boot to reveal a contorted face. 'What is that?' he asked taking a closer look as something caught his eye. A tiny string surrounded its neck at the end of which was attached a small black stone.

'It looks like a charm,' said Drake coming up behind him to have a look.

'A device of sorts,' added Wurt as he too came to examine the strange finding, 'it must be used to control the creature. We should destroy all of them.'

'Or at least get rid of them. We are strapped for time and that sky still looks dangerous to me. We do not want to be trapped on this ledge.' Drake had a point.

'Let's throw them from the mountain. These talismans are cold but it would probably be wiser to put some distance between them and us,' stated Dorian as he inspected another broken body nearby.

They instructed the remaining men and made quick work of tossing the bodies over the edge. A sombre mood fell upon the men as they went about the grisly task. The remorse at having lost two of their own was evident but there was no time to waste and before long, they were heading up the path and tending to their wounds as best they could.

THE ORACLE AT DORNE

By the time they reached the pass they found Fire and Brag settled amongst some trees. The storm finally broke. Wind and snow blew up the mountainside and caught them at their backs. They headed through the pass and into the rift and once they had navigated the highest point, they began to descend upon the plateau between the peaks. Here the weather began to calm.

Wurt took the lead, as this was his territory now. Nobody else had been this deep into Rega before. 'We shall soon come upon the mountain road,' he told them, 'I have taken this path many times. We will also be more protected between the peaks.'

'That is great news,' said Dorian, 'I was about to believe that we would be turned to statues of winter's glass.' He shivered and attempted to wrap the blanket he had donned more tightly about him. Everyone was doing the same, as the cold was almost unbearable with frosty daggers piercing the layers of cloth.

'It will not last, do not worry,' Wurt chided. 'It will subside as we descend further.'

Dorian was quite impressed for within minutes, the storm did indeed decrease in fervour, and soon they found themselves travelling through a still and markedly warmer wood. 'That is strange indeed,' he said, looking at Drake, 'how the weather has changed so suddenly. It is as if we have entered another realm.'

'You have entered another realm.' Wurt had that twinkle in his eye. 'This is really where the true Rega begins.'

'Where is Regavik from here?'

'Almost two days ride that way,' he answered pointing towards the northwest. There is another route through the mountains to the north, but this is the shortest way from Ravencroft.'

'Is that the route the Regan army will take?' asked Dorian with interest.

'I believe so,' answered Wurt, turning to him with a grin that illustrated his eagerness to join his brethren. 'This way is too tricky for an army. It will take them slightly longer but they will end up in the same place eventually. Hoth's Gate before Caledon is where we shall all come together.'

'Hopefully our venture won't take us too far off course,' commented Drake. 'We would want to get there in good time to meet our counterparts.'

'Yes we shall see,' agreed Dorian, 'I do not like this uncertainty. If only we knew exactly where we were going or at the very least, where we will be sent to.' He smiled at his friends who understood his meaning.

'Hopefully we will not be accosted by any more foul creatures,' said Wurt looking up at the skies. 'It is a pity we had to lose two good men.'

'I feel we are strangely protected here,' reassured Dorian, 'in any event I am certain the Tamulus will give us fair warning.' Dorian was concerned that somehow the bats might have relayed a message back to their puppet masters. Were their whereabouts divulged?

'It is good that the stone bonds with you Sire,' said Drake.

'Our quest will be bolstered once we find Disparager,' said Dorian feeling excited at the prospect. For the first time he felt a real confidence building within him. With the whole stone, he imagined he stood a chance against the evil intensifying in the north. He could feel it, a lingering menace that gained in strength with each passing day. It lay there at the periphery, waiting, biding its time. "When will it strike?" he thought.

They continued through the valley for most of the morning as the heavens above cleared to reveal a blue sky. The sudden change in the weather intrigued Dorian, from a winter blizzard to a spring day. "Two seasons in one morning," he thought, "this must surely be an enchanted wood."

They stopped to rest, eating a light lunch consisting of salted meat and biscuits. After lunch, they carried on towards the west, well into the afternoon. The trees here were gigantic and as they progressed along the path, the trees seemed to be getting ever larger. Dorian looked up at them and realised that he had never seen anything quite like it. 'These trees are incredible.'

'These are our homes,' said Wurt proudly.

'You live in the trees?' asked Dorian incredulously, 'I thought that dwarves lived in caves in the mountains.'

'You are mistaken, a common myth,' answered Wurt, 'we work in the caves and mine for ore and precious stones, but our homes are high in the trees. Only certain trees mind. These are the strong giant Regan Sequoias and Redwoods. They make marvellous homes.'

'I believe that some homes have been built to span more than one tree,' stated Drake.

'This is true. Some of my countrymen have built houses encompassing the tops of up to five trees.' Wurt looked very pleased with himself. 'Mine is constructed between three.'

'That is something I have to see,' said Dorian.

'Aye, you may yet my friend.' Wurt clicked his spurs, edging Daisy on ahead of them. 'We approach the lake.'

They followed Wurt for another league and eventually the trees gave way to an open expanse that held a beautiful lake. It was the lake Dorian had seen in his dream. The Sacred Wood lay on either side and in both directions; it rose into the mountains high above them. The water was blue and still and the party of men and horses did not waste time in reaching the edge to drink their fill.

'This water is pure and sweet,' noted Dorian filling his calfskins.

'This is the source of the Serpent's River and it feeds both Rega and Voltar. It is called Dorne,' said Wurt proudly.

'Truly a wonder,' Drake complimented.

'We shall pass on the eastern side,' instructed Wurt. 'That way is clear and will lead us to the dwelling place of the Oracle.'

They traversed on the side that Wurt had indicated and Dorian was in awe of the beauty of the place. Reeds shrouded the perimeter and banks of lilac irises adorned the edge. A flock of snow geese descended upon the surface not far from them and proceeded to wade gracefully, calling to each other as they sailed past. "It is like spring here," Dorian thought to himself.

About an hour later, they heard a strange sound, muted at first but then it grew to a rushing crescendo.

'What is it?' asked Dorian.

'The Serpent's Falls,' answered Wurt and with that, they rounded a bend to witness an exhilarating sight. Before them rose the most elegant waterfall. It fell from a great height in one strong column of water, crashing into a pool below and then cascading over layers of rock into the lake. 'It is said that this is where the first king of Rega did battle with a great dragon to claim these lands. They agreed upon a truce between monsters and men. Our ancestors made a decision that the dragons would have the peaks and we would have the valleys. An alliance of sorts, but they have left this world now and so it is that we live in peace with the land.'

'I have read about the ancient dragons of Rega,' Dorian offered his insights, 'but sadly none have been seen for centuries.'

'Aye, sad indeed,' Wurt lamented, 'we still tell fireside stories of what was and what could have been. There is an old fable about the first king riding on the back of his new ally. Whether there is any truth in this I do not know.'

'Where does the Oracle live?' asked Dorian looking around to see if he could spot a dwelling or any sign of life.

'We need to approach on foot from here and pass behind the falls. There is a clearing beyond those rocks on the other side. That is where we shall find her.'

They tied their horses to a small tree nearby and instructed the men to wait and keep guard. Drake and Wurt would accompany Dorian from here. With the bags of offerings slung over their shoulders, they began their crossing to the other side on foot. Moss covered the rocks, proving very slippery, and within minutes, they were drenched up to their knees. Once they found the passage that led behind the waterfall, they crept slowly along it with their backs to the glistening rock. When they emerged on the other side, they were soaked from head to toe. They laughed at the state they found themselves in but felt quite exhilarated by the whole experience. Wurt took them along a jagged path that climbed upwards and after much exertion; they finally arrived at the clearing he had mentioned. At the centre stood a large, elongated, level rock that looked like a table covered in a patchwork of grey and brown lichen.

'This is where we deposit our gifts,' said Wurt, as he offloaded his bag and emptied the contents onto the stone. Cups, plates and an assortment of trinkets fell out and the others followed his lead doing the same.

'And now what?' asked Dorian.

'And now we wait.'

'Oh, are we supposed to sit anywhere or just stand here out in the open? Where do we wait?' Dorian was concerned that it was all so informal. He looked about to see if there were any suitable rocks or logs that may serve as seats.

'We sit here,' said Wurt folding his legs beneath him and sitting on the grass.

'Oh I see,' Dorian lowered his body and found it awkward trying to mimic Wurt's posture.

The two men and the dwarf sat on the grass and waited. There was not much to say and so they sat in silence. They waited for about fifteen minutes and Dorian was about to say something when they heard a shrill voice cry out from the woods.

'A sparkle and a shine all glittering and all mine.'

They stood up to see a strange sight. Approaching from between the trees was an old woman. She was extremely short, even shorter than Wurt and hobbled over with the aid of a staff that was taller than she was. The Oracle was not speaking though. On her shoulder sat perched a magpie with twinkling eyes that darted from left to right.

'A sparkle I see and all mine,' it said again.

'All mine you mean,' said the old woman. She used the staff to measure her way forward, tapping the stone platform and coming to rest abreast of it. 'What have we here?' she asked, dropping the staff and reaching out for the pile of treasure that lay before her. Her wrinkled hands moved across the valuable objects feeling each one in turn. She was blind. 'Yes, Magenta,' she croaked, 'what do you see?'

The bird answered in that shrill voice, *'a sparkle, and a shine.'*

'Good girl,' chimed the old woman. Her face turned up to seek out the newcomers with closed eyes. 'Yes I am blind. Come here,' she beckoned.

Wurt pushed Dorian forward and he stumbled, having to right himself as he stepped closer to the Oracle.

'What do you see Magenta,' she asked.

'A boy, who would become a man,' was the magpie's answer.

'A prince who would become a king you mean,' stated the diminutive woman, 'stand closer my lord.'

Dorian moved around the stone table covered in riches. 'I am here Ma'am,' he said standing before her.

Her hands reached out for him and caught him at the elbows. 'Your face,' she whispered, 'I would see your face Sire.'

He bent down so that his face was on a level with hers, 'yes, ma'am.'

'A handsome face it is,' screeched Magenta bobbing up and down.

'So it is,' she agreed as her fingers worked his features and then in an instant she pulled at his shirt strings exposing the Tamulus. 'What do you see?'

'A sparkle and a glitter,' sang the magpie becoming excited. It jumped onto her head flapping its wings and then settled on her other shoulder stooping forward as if to peck at the stone.

'So you have it. The prophecy bears fruit,' she withdrew her spindly fingers, 'you seek the sword?'

'Yes, ma'am.'

'And what would you do when you have it? Hmm? Would you destroy the world? Rule the world?' Her voice had raised a few octaves.

'No. Ma'am I would regain my birthright,' he answered feeling annoyed.

'Ah, a prince after a throne,' she cackled and stepped back from him, 'yes I believe you. What does his heart look like Magenta?'

'No darkness, no light, but the future looks bright.'

'Yes and the light shall come for you my lord,' said the Oracle.

'I do not understand,' Dorian was confused.

'You will know my meaning before the battle is fought and won . . . or lost.'

'Will we win the battle?' he asked.

'That is up to you Sire.'

'Up to you,' shrieked Magenta.

'What must I do?'

'You must prove yourself worthy of the sword,' she answered going back to her loot.

'But where is the sword, please, I do not follow,' he was feeling bewildered by this exchange.

'Before I direct you, you must make me a promise; you must give me your word.'

'What is it ma'am?'

'You must bring your first born to me.' Her voice took on an ominous tone.

'I don't have any children,' he said sincerely.

'Don't now, but you will.'

'But you will,' echoed Magenta.

'What would you do with my child?' asked Dorian. He did not like the sound of these terms.

'I would not harm the child. I would merely bestow my blessing upon your offspring and present the infant with a gift from the forest.' She smiled and Dorian noticed she had no teeth. Whiskers sprouted from her chin and her tongue lolled in her mouth as she spoke.

'If those are your terms and you bear no malice towards me or any children that I may yet bear, I shall give you my word.'

'Those are not my full terms,' she cackled and he felt the urge to shake her.

'What more?' he asked calming himself.

'The silver.'

'Sparkle and shine,' croaked Magenta.

'Uh, yes of course.' He fished the pouch of silver coins from his pocket and presented it to her. 'But how did you know?'

She listened for the sound of coins tinkling and grabbed the bag of money as a sardonic smirk crossed her little face. 'I know more than you think,' she clucked at him. She weighed the bag in her hands and then moved it to her ear where she shook it to hear the jingle of the coins within. Magenta did a dance of victory on the other side. 'You must follow the eastern road from here up into the range and make your way to the Dragon's Peak. From there the stone will guide you to the caves above. You will find the Ajatar entrusted to guard the sword all these years. You must approach her on foot and alone. Only you can gaze upon her, anyone else will perish.' She began to pack her new acquisitions into the bags they brought.

'Thank you ma'am,' he said as he turned from her to join his companions who had been standing behind him in stony silence.

'Oh, I almost forgot . . .' she said.

He looked her way. 'Yes my Lady?'

'The innocent are virtuous, but they are tainted by this world.'

'Thank you,' he said, with a degree of uncertainty. He thought better than to ask for clarification as the Oracle was furiously packing her precious goods away. He decided he would let the cryptic message be. He guessed it would all make sense in good time.

TWENTY

DISPARAGER

Dorian and his companions made their way back behind the curtain of falling water and rejoined the men who waited with the horses. They were all curious as to what had happened. Wurt excitedly recounted the story of Dorian's encounter with the Oracle. There was a collective gasp and a few furtive glances between them as he mentioned the Ajatar.

'About that,' said Dorian, 'what exactly is the Ajatar?' He had never heard of this creature or person before.

'The Ajatar is the mother of all dragons,' answered Wurt. 'She is the fabled protector of serpents. Regan mythology speaks of her but I never believed she actually existed.'

'Anyone who looks at her is afflicted with disease. She spreads pestilence in her wake and is chained within the mountain,' said Drake, a look of worry in his face. There was a murmur amongst the men.

'Who chained her?' asked Dorian.

'The Regan King Kantor of old,' Wurt explained. 'With the Sacred Wood's blessing, he was entrusted with the task of forging the golden chains that finally entrapped her. He saved the people of Alton Savia from her wrath but paid a hefty price in return.'

'What happened?' Dorian remembered the Oracle telling him that he had to prove himself worthy of the sword; a thousand scenarios played out in his mind.

'The king was turned into a serpent and condemned to serve the Ajatar for eternity in compensation for her imprisonment.'

'By all the Gods! What of Disparager; how did that come to be in her possession?' This was not a very good story.

'One of King Kantor's descendants supposedly took a magical charm to her as a trade to free his ancestor's soul and to allow him a decent Regan burial.'

'And she accepted of course?'

'Yes she did; the charm was powerful, though it was not of her bloodline and she could not wield its power. She released King Kantor from the spell and he returned to his human form. The Ajatar left us nothing but bones and dust but at least he could have a royal burial and we could perform the rite of passage to free his spirit in thanks for his sacrifice. This all happened hundreds of years ago but it was the least we could do.' Wurt leaned against Daisy and folded his arms. Everyone else had gone deathly silent.

'But Wurt, if you knew all of this, why did you not tell us the tale before?' Dorian could not fathom the motive for Wurt's secrecy.

'I knew *of* the story but it has always been just a myth. A story told by nursemaids to naughty children. Nobody has ever believed it to be true and, moreover, there has been no inkling that the charm in question was in fact the sword, if it were true.' Daisy snorted behind him.

'Well it appears to be true now!' Dorian was annoyed. 'And what am I supposed to trade for the sword? I don't like this at all. She is probably going to ask me for my remaining children once the firstborn goes to the Oracle.'

Drake chuckled and said, 'I don't think the Oracle wants to harm anyone. I doubt this creature would ask that you sacrifice all of your children.'

'You don't know that, none of us do,' Dorian was surprised the Tamulus had not stirred at all. It was then that he realised all would be well. He already had one part of the Bloodstone in the Tamulus and the other half was rightfully his owing to his lineage. After all, the Ajatar's lot was merely to *guard* the sword, not become its owner.

'The Oracle would not send you to your death if she has made you promise something to her,' said Drake, matter-of-factly.

'That is true,' Wurt smiled, 'we will need to leave for the eastern road by first light. We do not want to find ourselves there by nightfall. We have not used that road for many years. It was used to access the mines up on Dragon's Peak and we abandoned those a generation ago.'

'This only gets better,' said Dorian with a hint of sarcasm. 'How far is it to the peak?'

'A few hours ride, provided the road is intact. We should make it by mid-morning tomorrow and, with any luck, we can be back down in time for a late lunch.'

'With a good dose of luck and Mia's blessing,' said Drake.

They spent the afternoon resting, washing their clothes, and bathing at the falls. Everyone was happy finally, to be rid of the blood and sweat and they made a fire to sit around as their clothes dried. After a meagre supper, they all collapsed into a deep slumber with the sound of the falls surging rhythmically behind them.

Drake woke everyone at first light and after a quick breakfast, the companions set out for the eastern road. They had to make their way through the forest, as there was no track leading from the lake. Wurt followed his nose and the rest of the party followed him faithfully. After about an hour, they reached the eastern road, which the Oracle had mentioned. Dorian could see that the road was unused for many years and that it had fallen into a bad state of disrepair. Strewn boulders, weeds, and bushes covered its length and breadth. In some places there were even trees growing in the middle of the road.

'This is going to be quite rough,' noted Drake as they began to pick their way between the debris.

'At least we have a path to follow,' retorted Wurt quite jovially. He really appeared to be enjoying this. 'Over yonder is where the road starts to climb. Look there, you can see as it winds uphill towards that peak.'

Dorian looked up to see a huge finger of black rock jutting into the sky just beyond the tree line ahead of them. Pockets of snow covered the rock and the summit was completely white. 'It looks like a dragon's head peeking out between the mountains.' He had never seen anything like it before and felt slightly intimidated by the immense size.

'Yes, hence the name,' said Wurt, 'it will be quite a climb. I can't believe that this is where Disparager lies after all this time. Who would have thought, right under our noses?' He spurred Daisy on and was the first to begin the ascent along the path that now began to zigzag uphill.

'How far up is the entrance to the caves?' asked Dorian mesmerized by the giddy tor before them.

'About an hour's climb,' answered Wurt. 'This path turns to stairs after a while and we will have to progress on foot from there. We will leave our horses at the first landing up ahead.'

'I think the rest of the men should wait there too. Perhaps you and Drake can accompany me to the entrance and I will continue from there alone. We must heed the Oracle's warning.'

'Aye, that is good with me. I shall not be entering those caves now that I know the truth that lurks within them,' Wurt was resolute.

'That sits well with me too,' Drake concurred.

'So be it,' agreed Dorian. Just then, he felt familiar warmth on his chest. 'The Tamulus speaks to me.'

'We must be getting closer,' noted Drake as he led Brag up the steep slope behind Daisy.

As they climbed, the stone at his chest began to get ever warmer until he thought it might scald his skin. This was strange; never before had he felt it get this hot. The sensations in the past were different. He could hear the men behind him talking about what lay ahead and there was a degree of trepidation in their voices.

They reached the landing as Wurt had foreseen and had to dismount. From here, a steep climb of stone steps angled upwards.

'This is where we shall leave you,' said Drake to the men, 'keep an eye out, and tend to the horses. It is a long ride back.'

They said farewell to each man clasping forearms in the Voltarian fashion and then headed up the stairs without further delay. The wind blew their cloaks about them as they climbed ever higher and Dorian was concerned that the prying eyes of the north may yet again seek them out. The Tamulus became unbearably hot and he had to free it from his skin and bring it out into the light of day. As he did so he was surprised to see, it shone with a bright red light.

'The stone has come to life,' said Wurt, noticing the reflection on the rocks around them, 'it is like a beacon, guiding you to your destiny.'

'It's a wonder,' said Drake fascinated by what he witnessed.

They reached the mouth of the cave and Drake and Wurt stood fast as Dorian made ready to enter. 'I take my leave of you now,' he said, 'wish me luck.'

'Go with the Gods,' said Wurt.

'Mia will protect you; after all, she has given you the Tamulus has she not?' Drake was confident.

Dorian said goodbye and began his sojourn alone into the gaping maw that lay before him. It was cold, dark, and wet but the Tamulus provided light enough for him to find his footing. The deeper he went, the brighter the stone became, but Dorian was still uncertain of his heading. He walked for what felt like an eternity along the tunnel that now bore downwards at a challenging gradient. Finally, he arrived at a large cavern and it appeared to be a crossroads of sorts as there were many tunnels leading from this central point.

'Where to now?' he asked aloud.

The Tamulus provided the answer as it had done in the past. He felt the familiar force ripple through his body and with it came a knowledge that he should move straight ahead. He continued along the tunnel, directly in front of him. He did not know what to expect, but knew that he was about to encounter something, for the Tamulus threw up visions of his arrival at the sword's guarded vault. It was then that he noticed another light ahead of him. The tunnel was drawing to a close and beyond it lay a massive cavern. He arrived through a small opening and found himself in front of an awe-inspiring sight.

On the ground some paces ahead was a stone pedestal and on top of that lay Disparager. It was an elegantly crafted long sword of steel, with an intricate pommel and a leather-bound grip, but most astonishing of all was the stone embedded in the cross guard. It was much larger than that of the Tamulus and beautifully cut, each of its facets casting candescent red shards of light across the walls of the cavern. As he stepped closer, both stones grew even brighter, as if they were one. He felt an incredible urge to take the sword in his hands.

'Breathtaking is it not?' said a whisper from the darkness.

'Who speaks to me?' he asked trying to search the shadows beyond the light of the stones.

'I am the Ajatar,' the voice was seductive. 'I am the keeper of the sword of Kings.'

'I am Dorian, successor to the throne of Arillon,' he introduced himself still searching for the speaker.

'I know who you are my lord,' she answered.

'Why do you not show yourself to me,' he asked.

'Men usually die in agony when they lay eyes upon my countenance. This is your test but it may be your undoing.' Her voice was provocative and sweet but he detected something else . . . deceit and danger.

'I am not afraid,' he said bravely. 'I have made it this far and I intend to take what is mine.'

'By *my* grace alone, I could have destroyed you the moment you set foot in my prison.'

'Why did you not?' he challenged.

'You have the Bloodstone. You are a true blood. I can feel your heart beating. It is strong and your intentions are pure. The sword has responded and accepted you; it yearns for the union with your amulet. Far be it from me to deny the stone of kings its destiny. I was enjoined to ensure this comes to pass.'

'So what is the test then;' his indignation was getting the better of him.

'It's quite simple really, I reveal myself to you, and if you are not afflicted with pestilence and live, you have passed the test.' A vile laugh slithered from her tongue.

'I am ready,' he said feeling both afraid and brave at the same time. The Tamulus bolstered his strength although it also painted a picture of a strange and foreboding power within the Ajatar.

'Ha, you may be ready, but is the world of men ready for what may be unleashed upon it? That is the question!'

It was then that he became aware of the movement around him. To the left and right and from above giant serpents surrounded him. They spun out of the darkness into the light of the stone. They were of many sizes and colours and writhed around him as one. They were in constant motion, turning and sliding, forming a prison of coils and scales that completely enclosed him. His heart was in his throat and his mouth went dry.

A woman's torso appeared from above, suspended at the arms by shining golden chains. A head emerged from the shadows to reveal a striking face, regal in its demeanour with bright green eyes that bore into him. Her hair was black and silky and fell across her chest screening her breasts. Her flesh was dark green in colour and scales appeared to cover her entirety. This was the extent of her human form, for from the waist down many snakes conjoined her and extended out from her. They were all a part of her; the image made Dorian shiver.

'So you are still alive, as I anticipated. Through the ages, many men have died by entering my domain. Your red charms protect you. Look at how they sing for you.' Was there an element of disdain in her words? Dorian was not sure.

'So what is to happen now my Lady? Does the fact that I live and I am unafflicted by disease permit me to leave with Disparager?'

'You will leave with Disparager, but I would have you stay awhile. I have not entertained a guest for many years and I yearn for company.'

Dorian did not feel the urge to remain in her presence any longer than was necessary and was about to refuse when he realised this may not be the wisest path. 'What would you have of me?' he asked.

'Conversation my lord, I would ask you questions of the world outside. Will you grant me this request?'

'As you wish,' he agreed.

They spent many hours talking and Dorian found that he was able to answer most of the Ajatar's questions without any problem. She was particularly interested in the history of the three kingdoms; however, he felt that his memory did not serve him as well as it should have under the circumstances. The Ajatar did not seem to mind and asked him of matters that were more mundane in nature. He found this quite odd but said nothing of it until finally her curiosity seemed to be satisfied.

'Thank you Dorian of Arillon, I ask you for one more token of your goodwill before I release the weapon into your hands.'

'If I can meet your demand I shall gladly do it,' he said, glad to be alive and feeling a lot better about how this encounter was unfolding. It crossed his mind that this was a second day of pacts.

'Swear an oath before my minions,' she continued.

'If it is something I can uphold I shall swear it.'

'Promise to spare the life of my progeny and release any from the tie that binds them. This is well within your power,' she requested cocking her head and for the first time revealing ophidian fangs.

Her eyes dazzled him and he felt for an instant that their beauty was drawing him in. He had to pull himself away to think about this request for a moment. He did not quite understand what she meant but decided that sparing the life of a serpent was well worth her favour.

'I swear this to you, that I shall spare the life of any serpent that bears me no ill will.'

'Use the powers at your disposal to free them. The malice that any of my children may display would not be of their own will, but that of the hand that enslaves them.'

Dorian realised what she meant. 'The hand of Mur?' he asked.

'It is the hand of destruction and enslavement,' she said, 'beware the blood of your father's house that seeks to destroy you and enslave the entire world.'

Dorian blanched as he realised the full implication of her words. The weight of responsibility lay heavy upon him but he turned his attention to the Ajatar. 'And what of you my Lady, will you always be imprisoned so?' asked Dorian with empathy for her fate.

'I have waited a very long time for this day and am now glad to be rid of this burden. It has pained and saddened me that I have been unable to quicken the stone. A deceptive quarry it has proven to be. This release will not free me for I am yet bound by an old spell from another time.'

'Will you ever be free?'

'I may yet see the light of day. My fate lies in the hands of the elder Gods, but I am content for now. Thank you Dorian of Arillon and remember your oath.' Within seconds, the Ajatar withdrew leaving him alone with Disparager.

He wiped the sweat from his brow and stepped forward to lay his hand upon the hilt. A last blinding flash of crimson light erupted from both stones as he held Disparager aloft. He felt a rush of strength coarse through his veins and a thousand images flick through his mind as the emanation subsided. He witnessed the rise and fall of empires and kings, spied a thousand battles and peered through the window into the many lives that were lived and lost in congruity with the life of the sword. The Bloodstone had settled as one with him. In that moment, he understood exactly who he was. His chosen path was clear. He was the king of Arillon, saviour and master of Alton Savia and the bearer of the light that would sweep away the darkness.

Dorian emerged from the cave in the late afternoon bearing Disparager on his back. Drake and Wurt were ecstatic and shouted in victory but this was nothing in comparison to the roar let out by the men once Dorian and his friends descended and he held the sword aloft before them.

'Victory is not yet ours,' said Dorian sternly after the celebratory whoops had subsided. 'We shall make haste, returning to Morgan the Free and our brothers in Ravencroft, and then onwards into the gap to join the armies of Rega and Voltar. There is a storm approaching the likes of which our generation has never seen. The time has come to return balance, dignity, and justice to our beloved Alton Savia.'

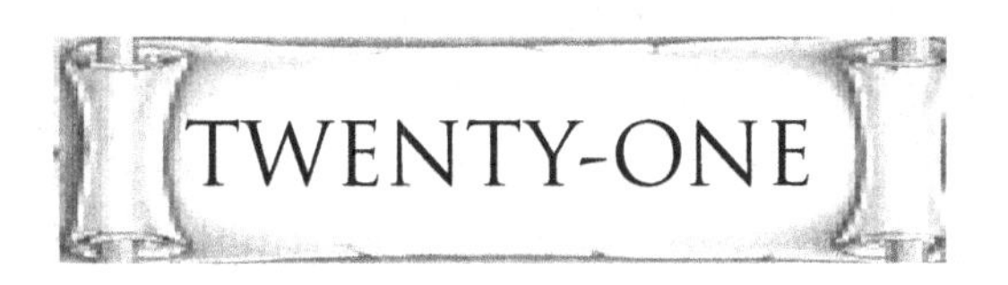

KINGS' COUNCIL

Gwyneth stood in front of her pavilion and looked out at her father's army positioned along both sides of the valley. She had been unable to sleep, with unpleasant dreams assailing her throughout the night. Her thoughts now dwelt upon her conversation with the Dryad. The encounter had unsettled her. What had the tree spirit meant by her prophecies? It was with difficulty that she convinced her father of her story and if it had not been for Goran, who vaguely remembered the incident, the king would have cast her revelation aside as a fanciful yarn. Fortunately, her father's army was now safely camped alongside that of King Mogador within the confines of the Sacred Wood. He had been extremely angry that they had lost the element of surprise and that somehow, Tarrant and the Blackwraith had passed them without notice to give the game away.

A scattering of stars hung suspended in a black limbo above her. Dawn broke slowly over the eastern escarpment with the faint light already visible. The barking dogs broke the forest silence and the angry shouts from the men attempting to quiet them amused Gwyneth. The soldiers did not take kindly to the unruly canines violating their slumber.

'Can't sleep either I see,' sounded a voice from the dark. Gwyneth turned to see Goran walking towards her.

'Yes, bad dreams,' she stated, 'what about you my captain.'

'Restless. Waiting around like this makes me feel like a Jack-in-the-box,' he ran his fingers through his hair trying to tame a few wayward curls.

Gwyneth looked at him as he stood beside her. He adopted her pose and turned his face skywards. She could not imagine him in a box; he was far too big and ungainly. 'I believe we have received word that the true heir to the throne of Arillon arrives today,' she said.

'Yes, the lookout has sent word that his party approaches the Drakenstein as we speak,' he added. 'I have heard that the young prince has found the sword.'

Her eyes widened with excitement. 'Yes, my father informed me of this development yesterday. He received word from Ravencroft that Morgan too accompanies the prince. This makes me feel a lot more confident considering the northern forces are massing on the plains below us.'

'As I see it we stand a good chance of defeating that mad bastard and his consort, even though their forces swell in numbers. Having King Mogador's army by our side certainly helps our cause,' Goran sounded hopeful.

'Yes indeed,' she too wished for victory. 'Our spies tell us that the forces of Arillon still pledging allegiance to Dragar have set up camp just beyond the forest a few leagues from our position. They have also witnessed a mobilization of forces from Mur. Many warships have landed at Karn and the enemy has overrun the city. I worry for the people there withstanding the worst of this barbarian plague. Many refugees have been seen pouring southwards.' A look of despair accompanied her words.

'The Murian contingent will be upon us soon,' said Goran with a sigh that sent a cloud of misty breath before him. 'We don't have much time to prepare. I am interested to find out what your father's strategy will be.'

'Yes, I too am intrigued. The conference with King Mogador on this matter over breakfast will be very enlightening.'

'Have you heard more of the Murian forces? I have heard some disturbing rumours of strange weaponry and large beasts that are ridden by iron-clad warriors.'

'Yes, my stomach turns at the thought of their cruelty towards the innocent in their path. There are horrendous tales of people being attacked and eaten alive by these creatures.' Gwyneth turned away from him and studied the horizon as the ominous light of dawn crept over the mountains and sent probing fingers into the woods. The encampment was coming to life.

'We should make ready for the meeting with your father,' said Goran, 'I need a hearty meal to prepare me for this day.'

They retired to their tents and made ready for the day. There was a hubbub of activity by the time Gwyneth reappeared wearing the armour found for her at her father's bidding. Men could not prevent themselves from looking at her as she made a fine sight in her silver chainmail and breastplate. Her amber hair looked beautifully stark in contrast to the blue and white colours of her Voltarian cape. Her eyes too were striking as she flashed a smile at the passersby who ogled her. "What on Earth are they staring at," she thought as she made her way to her father's precinct.

'Ah, a sight for tired old eyes,' her father declared as she entered his spacious marquee. 'I would never have thought that the sight of a woman in armour could make one's soul soar, albeit my daughter at arms.' A murmur of agreement from the many officers who sat at the king's table rumbled through the room.

'I think the enemy would fall foul of such a paragon of Voltarian might.' King Mogador spoke and the response from his men was even more agreeable. They rose as Gwyneth took her seat beside her father. This was the first time she had met the king of Rega and he intrigued her. He had arrived late the previous day and she had missed the fanfare, rather accompanying Goran on a tour of the further reaches of the camp. He was not a typical Regan dwarf as he stood a clear head above the others. He sported a large, black beard that grew from his chin in many shining curls. He wore a tunic in the purple and black colours of the mountain kingdom and polished bronze armour that clad most of his body.

'Thank you for your complimentary words of praise and support,' said King William, 'let us give thanks to Mia.' He called forth a young, newly assigned priest to the affairs of faith and the spiritual wellbeing of the Voltarian forces.

Liam approached in his raw cotton habit. 'In Mia we trust and we thank her for the bountiful blessings she has bestowed upon us.'

'In Mia we trust,' was the combined reply from the gathering.

Breakfast was a noisy affair with the usual banter as everyone discussed the troubles facing them. Bryn sat beside Goran, waiting for the scraps that his master threw to him.

'Is the welcoming party ready for Prince Dorian?' asked King William of one of his aides.

'Yes Sire, everything is in place. The men will be waiting for your emissary up at Hoth's Gate.'

'Good, we should move our archers and footmen down the valley to cover the approach to our encampment. We have new intelligence that the Murians have already passed through Folkestone and will meet with Dragar's forces later today.' There was a rumble from the officers as they realised the gravity of the situation.

'This is worse than we thought,' said Goran his hand stroking Bryn's head.

'Indeed,' responded King William, 'Folkestone has been sacked and looted and there has been much loss of life. The forces within Arillon who stand opposed to Dragar are reportedly gathering in the east. We have sent word for them to take the southern road through the hills and join the fray on the enemy's eastern flank when the time comes. We have sent an advance party to guide them.'

'Rega stands by your side King William,' said Mogador, 'my men accompany yours on that mission and will fight to the death.'

'Thank you my friend,' said King William.

'How will we counter the bloodthirsty creatures they are purported to drive before their army?' asked Gwyneth.

'This is something we need to consider. We shall take council on this and other matters with King Mogador and his captains. Until we find an answer let us ensure our soldiers are ready for any attack on our position.' King William revised his strategy with his captains delegating the many responsibilities that would ensure the mobilisation went smoothly. King William concluded breakfast and everyone stirred to action while he retired to his quarters with his Regan counterpart. Gwyneth and Goran were to move up the valley to welcome the incumbent young king of Arillon and then escort him to meet the kings of Voltar and Rega.

At midday, the welcoming party reached the gap known as Hoth's Gate further up the valley. Huge slabs of granite, hewn from the mountains by men of old, marked the entrance into the valley and the standards of Voltar and Rega now ranged between them. The strong wind that sprang up from the plains below ravaged the flags. Gwyneth did not like the odour that came with it, it was rank, and she was certain the smell of death lingered in her nostrils. 'A foul smell rises on this wind,' she noted to Goran.

'I can smell it too,' he agreed, 'the smell of death and blood.'

Just then a field horn sounded above them and word came that the members of the Brotherhood approached. Gwyneth and Goran moved to their positions atop their great steeds and peered up the path to witness the arrival. There was a cheer up ahead as the men from Ravencroft crested the hill and passed through the gap into the valley. Gwyneth noticed Morgan among the company of riders, as well as some other familiar faces. However, the sight of the handsome, blonde, young man who rode beside Morgan astounded her. This was clearly the future king of Arillon as he glowed with an understated confidence and his eyes held a powerful resolve. More than that, it was the mighty sword at his back that marked his status among his compatriots, for it glimmered with a silver magnificence. At its hilt, a red stone's many facets caught the sun and sent a ripple of wonder through the onlookers. "That must be the fabled Bloodstone," she thought.

The arriving party dismounted and joined Gwyneth under the royal pergola. Morgan stepped forward to complete the formalities, 'my Lady, Princess Gwyneth of Voltar may I present Prince Dorian, heir to the throne of Arillon.'

Dorian bowed uncomfortably as he was not accustomed to court etiquette, but remembered some of the lessons Morgan had taught him. 'My Lady,' he said, 'it is my pleasure to make your acquaintance.'

Gwyneth curtsied and responded, 'my Lord Dorian, the House of Voltar welcomes you and we offer our humble hospitality under the circumstances. You must be tired and thirsty, let us have a drop of wine, and then make our way to my father's quarters.'

'These are my brothers in arms, Drake and Flynn Arvin of Arillon; they have been instrumental in bringing Prince Dorian to us,' said Morgan as the brothers stepped forward to meet Gwyneth.

'Well met gentlemen, any brother of Morgan the Free is a brother of mine.' She smiled graciously and remembered these two men from another time, in her father's court, when she was much younger.

'Flynn has recently survived an ordeal with a Blackwraith, he nearly lost his life in the service of the Brotherhood,' added Morgan.

'I have heard of this misfortune and your brave recovery from my father,' she said to Flynn and then turning to Morgan, 'and I believe it was thanks to your powers that our friend here was brought back from the brink of eternity.'

'It was Prince Dorian who saved him really, but only the strong could survive something like that,' offered Morgan. He turned to introduce Wurt, 'and this is Wurt of Rega.'

The dwarf jumped forward eagerly and bowed with a flourish saying, 'my Lady Gwyneth, it is my pleasure. Word of your beauty and grace has long since reached the mountains of Rega.'

'Why Mr. Wurt, you are most kind,' she retorted with a blush. The other men looked at each other with a smirk while Drake elbowed Flynn in the side.

After the introductions, Gwyneth and her first captain accompanied the group to meet her father and King Mogador. Gwyneth could not prevent herself from taking in as much of the young prince as she possibly could. She could not put her finger on something about him. As they made their way down the valley, they quietly discussed rather polite and mundane matters, such as the weather and the natural beauty of the valley. The afternoon sun caught Dorian's face at an angle making his hazel eyes shine as he looked at her. His fine features struck her as much his free spirit and quiet strength did. It was in that moment that she felt something stir deep within her; a yearning that she had never experienced before. It was as if she had been waiting for this moment her entire life and somehow their destinies entwined in an inexplicable way. The words spoken by the Dryad entered her mind and she realised now what the sylvan spirit had meant. This young king-in-waiting would be hers.

There was a wonderful celebration when the men of the Brotherhood from Ravencroft were presented to the kings of Voltar and Rega. Word spread throughout the camp and the jubilation reached from Hoth's Gate right down to the plains of Caledon. It was during this outpouring of emotion that a young boy made his way up the valley as if in a trance. He went unnoticed by any of the lookouts or soldiers as they took him to be one of their own. Eventually he found his way to the council of kings and slipped under the striped fabric of the main marquee, to stand among the men who gathered around the war table.

Dorian sat at the makeshift war table in the presence of King William and King Mogador, with Morgan at his right hand side and the brothers from Arillon on his left. Wurt sat with the officers that had accompanied the Ravencroft contingent watching the proceedings keenly.

'It is an honour to be in the company of men who have the best interests of Alton Savia at heart,' said King William. 'The enemy is at our gates. Our spies tell us that the Murians have dispatched a formidable army. The plains below us are crawling with outlandish beasts of war and they stand firm with Dragar's forces. A full-scale assault on our position is imminent. The time has come for us to put our heads together and formulate a strategy to win this war.'

There was a rumble of agreement. King Mogador raised his hand to calm the assembly, 'we are pleased that Prince Dorian has found his way to stand with us.' There was a cheer and Dorian bowed his head in gratitude. 'Our hero has found Disparager and delivered the Bloodstone to reinforce our cause.' Another cheer erupted and the king of the dwarves raised his hand again to tame the response. 'The prophecy reaches fulfilment and in line with the conventions of our mutual heritage we pledge our allegiance to the true king of Arillon.' This elicited a tumult of euphoria.

Dorian rose to his feet and then bowed gracefully saying, 'I thank you for these words of support and . . .' It was then that he felt it.

The Tamulus spoke to him, imparting a sense of danger and dread. Someone nearby intended him harm but the message was confused as he became aware of an evil entity that masked a vulnerability and innocence.

Morgan felt it too and pointed towards a group of men standing nearby, 'THERE,' he shouted, 'beware, something vile has penetrated our ranks.'

The men in the vicinity he indicated fell back in horror to expose Jeb standing alone. Wurt immediately lunged forward, dagger in hand towards the intruder.

'WAIT!' shouted Dorian. He was aware of the child's innocence and sensed a dark presence within him using the child as a vehicle to convey its intentions. An evil force trapped the child, holding its captor by means of a crude obsidian talisman at the boy's throat. Dorian could feel this instrument of Mur weighing the boy down and manipulating him. He drew Disparager from its sheath at his back and plunged the tip into the earth before him. The eye of Disparager burst to life and cast a crimson light over the boy and the space surrounding him. 'This child is under the influence of Gordus Murdim. Let him be!'

Wurt stood down faithfully.

Everyone else now stood well back from the boy who was clearly under the influence of some sinister force. 'Speak!' commanded Dorian.

'Are you the bearer of the stone?' asked the boy.

'Yes, I am Dorian of Arillon, bearer of the Bloodstone.'

The young boy's eyes rolled back showing only the whites and his body splayed as if drawn by invisible chains that pulled at his arms and legs.

'Be warned, mongrel dog! You are no match for my powers,' screamed a voice which came out of Jeb's mouth, but it was not his own this time. It was a male voice, shrill and threatening. *'You and your flock will fall at the hands of my armies!'*

A collective gasp escaped from the mouths of the gathered men as they all took another step back in trepidation. None of them had ever witnessed such a thing.

'Who are you?' demanded Dorian.

'I am the Gatekeeper of Mur,' answered the voice.

'What do you want?' boomed Dorian.

'You will kneel before the might of Mur and relinquish your claim to the throne of Arillon.'

'And if I will not?'

'Then you will feel my wrath and wish that you had never been born,' howled the voice.

'You are a coward,' said Dorian, 'hiding inside an innocent child. You should be ashamed!'

A shout of defiance rang out from the host of soldiers.

'This is but a vessel,' uttered the voice with menace, *'we have taken many more and will take more still. The power of Mur is greater than you imagine and we have the means to crush you and your pathetic allies!'*

Dorian felt the menacing force draining the lifeblood from the poor child. The power beyond the talisman was drawing the boy's living spirit towards a dark and perilous abyss. It was attempting to steal the child's soul. He had to act quickly to prevent the evil entity from snuffing out the young boy's life like a candle. Dorian's anger rose up like a tidal wave. It swelled within him, gaining momentum; however, he constrained it into a single thread of energy through the Tamulus. The eye of Disparager focussed his measured rage, which he then released through the portal by which the entity controlled the young boy.

There was an awful shriek as the power of the unified Bloodstone sprang first from the Tamulus and then through the eye of the sword in an arcing, red, needle of light. It connected with the amulet around the boy's neck obliterating it instantly. Shards of black stone spun through the air as they were incinerated, leaving a foul smell of sulphur behind. The child fell limply to the ground as the true king of Arillon dispatched his possessor.

'Let that be a lesson to you, creature of darkness!' shouted Wurt triumphantly as a cheer rent the air.

Dorian went to the young child's side and knelt down to lift him in his arms. The colour had returned to the boy's face and he opened his eyes. 'What happened? Who are you?' he asked, looking at Dorian in fear.

'You are safe now my lad. I am Dorian, the King of Arillon, what is your name?'

'My name is Jeb Sire,' said the boy, attempting a smile before he fell into a deep slumber.

INDEX OF NAMES

Ajatar—The mother of Serpents
Alton Savia—Region consisting of the three kingdoms
Amphithere—Snake-like dragon
Aral River—River running through Arillon
Arillon—First kingdom of Alton Savia
Barnabas—a guard in Voltar
Barton Woodruff—Baron of Graven
Black Tower—Tallest tower in Graven Keep
Bloodstone—Fabled magical stone
Bo—One of Kruger's gang members
Borratar—Historical mage of the South
Borrowed River—River running through Voltar
Brag—Drake's horse
Breeze—Princess Gwyneth's horse
Bryn—Goran's wolfhound
Buttons—One of Kruger's gang members
Calavaria—Palace in Caledon and seat of the throne
Caledon—Capital of Arillon
Cape of Storms—Southern point of Voltar
Celestria—Regan Dryad
Daisy—Wurt's Regan pony
Disparager—Mystical ancient sword

Dorian Arillon—Heir to the throne of Arillon
Dorne—Regan Lake and home of the Oracle
Dragar Arillon—Half brother to King Gordon
Dragon's Peak—A mountain of Rega
Drake Arvin—Member of the Brotherhood
Drakenstein—Regan mountain range
Drax—Murian slave trader
Druid's End—Small town in Voltar
Fire—A black stallion given to Dorian by the Baron
Flynn Arvin—Member of the Brotherhood
Folkestone—Town in Arillon
Goran Wilbur-axe—A captain of Voltar
Gothar—Regan town
Gratin—One of Kruger's gang members
Graven—Town in Voltar
Great Arch—Bridge between Voltar and Rega
Gwyneth Cairn—Princess of Voltar
Hoth's Gate—Regan mountain pass
Houndsteeth—Voltarian mountain pass
Ishtar—City in Kalvar
Jeb—One of Kruger's gang members
Johnny—One of Kruger's gang members
Kalvar—Country west of Rega
Kandor—Coastal city in Mur
Kantor—Old King of Rega
Karn—Coastal city in Arillon
Krillafax—Amphithere of Mur
Kruger—Leader of a gang
Laurel—Town in Arillon
Liam—Voltarian priest
Maggot—Innkeeper and criminal
Marion—Butcher's wife in Graven
Mark—Voltarian Scout

Mia—The Earth-Goddess
Miss Lambourne—Tutor from Graven
Mogador—King of Rega
Morgan the Free—Leader of the Brotherhood
Mur—Northern country
Muria—Capital of Mur
Murian Strait—Northern Sea
Oonagh—Servant of Arillon
Owen Barclay—Dorian's adopted uncle
Ravencroft—Seat of the Brotherhood of Guardians
Rea—Town in Mur
Rega—Western Kingdom of Alton Savia
Regavik—Capital of Rega
Rudder—Owen's donkey
Ruth—Owen's wife
Sacred Wood—Regan magical forest
Sara—One of Kruger's gang members
Serpent's River—River running through Rega
Shram—Servant of Lord Tarrant
Smithfield—Town in Arillon
Southern Ocean—Ocean to the south
Tamulus—Mystical ancient amulet
Tarash—Capital of Traal
Tarrant—Prelate of Arillon
The Badlands—Western region of Voltar
The Mermaid Inn—Maggot's Inn
The Weary Traveller—Owen's Inn
Toby Barclay—Owen's son
Traal—Western country
Voltar—Southern Kingdom of Alton Savia
Voltar Regis—Capital of Voltar
William Cairn—King of Voltar
Wurt—Regan soldier and ranger